# THE MYSTERY
# ON ALASKA'S
# Iditarod
# Trail

First Edition ©2003 Carole Marsh/Gallopade International/Peachtree City, GA
Current Edition ©August 2015
Ebook Edition ©2011
All rights reserved.
Manufactured in Peachtree City, GA

Carole Marsh Mysteries™ and its skull colophon are the property of Carole Marsh and Gallopade International.

Published by Gallopade International/Carole Marsh Books. Printed in the United States of America.

Editor: Jenny Corsey
Editoial Assistant: Carrie Runnals
Cover Design: Vicki DeJoy
Picture Credits: Amanda McCutcheon
Content Design: Steven St. Laurent, Lynette Rowe

Gallopade International is introducing SAT words that kids need to know in each new book that we publish. The SAT words are bold in the story. Look for this special logo beside each word in the glossary. Happy Learning!

Gallopade is proud to be a member and supporter of these educational organizations and associations:

**American Booksellers Association**
**American Library Association**
**International Reading Association**
**National Association for Gifted Children**
**The National School Supply and Equipment Association**
**The National Council for the Social Studies**
**Museum Store Association**
**Association of Partners for Public Lands**
**Association of Booksellers for Children**
**Association for the Study of African American Life and History**
**National Alliance of Black School Educators**

*Once upon a time...*

Hmm, kids keep asking me to write a mystery book. What shall I do?

Write one about spiders!

On the *Mystery Girl* airplane ...

I CAN FLY US ANYWHERE!

Or aboard the *Mimi!*

Take me to the Forbidden City!

Or by surfboard, rickshaw, motorbike, camel ...

All great ideas! I can put a lot of history, MYSTERY, legend, lore, and laughs in the books! We can use other boys and girls in the books. It will be educational and fun!

Good stuff!

The *Mystery Girl* is all revved up—let's go!

You mean now?

## LET'S GO!

*Mystery Girl*

And so, Mimi, Papa, Christina, and Grant took off aboard the *Mystery Girl* and America's National Mystery Book Series—where the adventure is real and so are the characters! —was born.

## START YOUR ADVENTURE TODAY!

READ THE BOOK!

GO ONLINE!

TRACK YOUR ADVENTURES!

APPLY TO BE A CHARACTER!

Yikes! That was close!

Rats!

# ABOUT THE CHARACTERS

Christina
Yother
Age 9

Grant
Yother
Age 7

Carolina
Windham
Age 11

Oliver
Watkins
Age 7

Meeting a Malamute!

# 1
# A LONG WAY FROM HOME

Christina was so excited to get out of school for yet another trip with her grandparents and little brother, Grant, who was seven. She was nine years old and in fourth grade and though she loved school, she always found the 'real' world much more interesting. Her grandmother, Mimi, wrote mystery books and always took Christina and Grant along when she went on trips to do research about her books. It seemed that most every time, Christina and Grant would get into some sort of mystery themselves–giving Mimi even more to write about!

This trip promised to be one of the most exciting yet. Mimi was taking them to Alaska, 'The Last **Frontier**.' She was writing a book about the world's most famous dog sled race, the Iditarod.

They had all awakened very early that morning, while it was still dark outside, left

Peachtree City–where they lived, and flew out of Atlanta's Hartsfield International airport. Their flight to Seattle, Washington took about five hours where they had a layover before leaving for Anchorage. Christina had to set her Carole Marsh Mysteries watch back three hours to make up for the time difference between Georgia and Seattle.

A layover is just another word for 'hurry up and wait,' Christina thought. It sure seems to take a long time to get anywhere on the big commercial airlines. You have to *wait* in so many lines and *wait* to be called to find your seat on the airplane and then *wait* for the flight attendants to show you the safety rules and then *wait* until the pilot starts the engines and then *wait* your turn on the runway before you ever even get a chance to get off the ground.

Christina liked flying in her grandfather's little red plane, *My Girl*, much better. But *My Girl* would never make it all the way to Alaska. "So, a girl has to do, what a girl has to do," Christina said aloud to herself.

They hardly had time to get settled in their seats for the last leg of the trip before Grant whined, "When are we going to get there? We've been flying for *days*."

"Grant, please stop complaining," said Mimi from across the aisle. "I know hours seem like days when you're on an airplane, but we've only got a little while before we land in Anchorage and then we'll be on a whole new adventure. I promise it will be well worth the wait."

"Let's ask the flight attendant for some more munchies," Christina suggested.

Christina and Grant crunched on pretzels and snack mix and gulped bottomless cups of lemonade, as they watched a movie and played card games of Crazy Eights. They giggled at Mimi and Papa as their heads bobbed in tandem, snores erupting from their open mouths.

"This is going to be so cool," Grant whispered in Christina's ear, so as not to wake Mimi and Papa. "We get to explore Alaska and go to the Iditarod."

"Yeah, but Mimi's going to have the most fun," Christina said sulking. "She actually gets to ride along with a musher on the Iditarod Trail in the real race and write about her experience. She's *sooooo* lucky."

"Musher? What's that?" asked Grant, "Sounds like that squishy stuff with the marshmallows that Aunt Cassidy makes on Thanksgiving."

"Ha, ha, very funny." Christina scolded, "You know it's the person who drives the dog sled in the races. But, I bet you *didn't* know that dog sled racing is the official state sport of Alaska," Christina added.

"You always have to know everything, don't you?" Grant grumbled.

"Oh, Grant," Christina said. "I'm just kidding with you."

"Okay," said Grant. "But I bet you didn't know that Libby Riddles was the first woman to win the Iditarod, in 1985!" He pumped up his chest like a proud rooster and tucked Mimi's *My First Pocket Guide: Alaska* behind his back so his sister couldn't see it.

"That may be true," said Christina. "But, Susan Butcher is a four-time winner and the first person *ever* to win three Iditarod races in a row."

"Oh, you think you are so smart. But, did you know that the capital of Alaska is Juneau?" Grant asked.

"I know, but do Ju-neau?" Christina popped back.

"You are so funny, I forgot to laugh," Grant said, as they both broke into giggles.

A loud snore escaped from Papa's mouth, and the children erupted in laugher.

Mimi snorted awake. "What are you two laughing about?" she asked.

"Oh nothing," Christina said, sneaking a knowing glance at Grant. They both covered their mouths with their hands, unsuccessfully stifling their laughter.

"We will be starting our descent into Anchorage momentarily," the pilot's voice announced over their heads, distracting Mimi just in time.

Christina looked over Grant's shoulder through the small oval-shaped airplane window. She could see the peaks of snow-covered mountains and the telltale aqua blue of glaciers. The sky was clear with billowy clouds that looked like the fluffy cotton that she pulled from the hole in her pillow at night when she couldn't sleep.

"Oh, great!" shouted Grant. "We're here. We're here! I thought this day would never come."

"You mean hour, right?" Christina corrected.

"Whatever," Grant answered, too excited to quarrel.

As the airplane taxied in from the runway, the children fidgeted in their seats in anticipation. Mimi and Papa gathered their things, picking up wayward playing cards, papers, and markers from under the seats.

"Be sure to set your watches one hour behind," instructed the pilot. "You are now on Alaska Time," his voice sounded smiley to Christina as she moved the hands of her watch backwards until another hour was erased. Wouldn't it be great to do this whenever you wanted? You could just keep resetting your watch and play as long as you liked, Christina thought.

When the airplane came to a complete stop, Grant and Christina waited until they heard the bell that indicated it was safe to unbuckle their seatbelts. Then they scrambled for their carry-on luggage. Once Mimi was sure they had all their belongings, they stepped into the aisle and followed the other passengers to the front of the plane. More *waiting*, thought Christina.

Finally, they disembarked, thanking the pilot as they stepped off the airplane.

"Have a wonderful stay in Alaska," the pilot said.

"Oh, we will," Mimi said, "We always have fun wherever we go. It's just part of having grandchildren."

As they stepped though the passageway, the cold air hit them square in the face. They would need to unpack their warm winter outfits as soon as they got the rest of their luggage from the baggage claim.

Christina had the feeling of being in another country as she walked through the airport with Mimi and Papa and Grant. She stared at the people around her. She'd never seen so many parkas and flannel shirts in her life. Not to mention all the slushy dripping boots, snowsuits, hats, and gloves—it all seemed so strange.

Christina couldn't help but think they were in for a great adventure. A *mysterious* adventure, most likely, if this trip turned out to be anything like the other trips they'd been on with Mimi and Papa. Though this one would no doubt be the coldest of them all. *Brrr!*

They walked through the airport, chatting excitedly about the newness of everything. Just a few paces behind followed a tall, dark-haired man with a moustache, matching them step for step being very careful *not* to be noticed!

# 2
# GOLD DUST SOUP

The drive from the airport to the hotel was short but boasted beautiful scenery. The rocky mountains towered into the sky, capped with icy white frosting like one of Mimi's yummy cupcakes.

Papa had rented a SUV, so they could all sit comfortably and have room for all the luggage. It took a lot more suitcases to carry winter clothes than it did their usual attire of t-shirts and shorts. Plus, the SUV had the four-wheel drive they needed to get through the ice and snow.

After they settled into the Gold Rush Hotel, with its historical gold nuggets displayed in the lobby, Mimi, Papa, Christina, and Grant set out to find a place to eat. They decided to take a stroll through Anchorage and show off the warm snow boots and parkas that Mimi had mail-ordered from a catalog. No one in Georgia sold snow boots or parkas in March or any other time, for that matter.

The snow crunched under their feet. It hardly ever snowed in Georgia. If it did, it would melt almost as fast as it hit the ground, so this knee-deep stuff was new and exciting. Grant stomped up and down with each step, making loud cracking noises as the icy surface broke under his feet.

"I'm sure glad we brought these parkas." Mimi said with a shiver, as she wrapped her red fur-lined hood more tightly around her neck. The wind blew over the streets causing sheets of fine powder to rush past them, like sand blowing off the dunes on a **blustery** spring day at the beach. *Only a whole lot colder!*

"Papa, I thought you said it was going to be dark here most of the day," Christina said, squinting from the bright sun.

"Yes, but that's not until we get further north," Papa said. "Here, in Anchorage in March, they have about twelve hours of daylight. As we get closer to Nome it will be less and less. I think Nome has about five hours of daylight a day."

"Yuck!" Grant said. "Those kids must feel like moles playing in the dark all day."

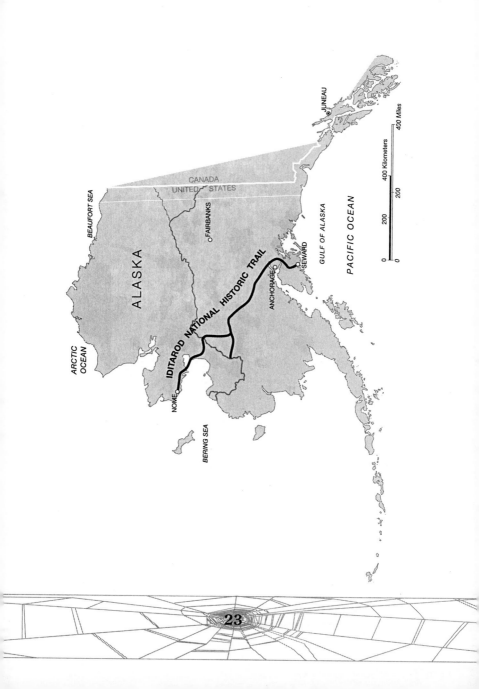

"Well, I'm sure they're used to it," Papa said. "They really don't have a choice."

"In the summertime, the sun barely even goes down," Mimi said.

*Wow!* Now that would be great fun, Christina thought. She wished that they had come in the summer. It would be really cool to have daylight for almost twenty-four hours. You could play outside all night long. On second thought, then they'd miss the Iditarod.

"Yes, wouldn't it be wonderful to be able to fish or play golf until three o'clock in the morning?" Papa said.

The kids laughed in agreement, but Mimi rolled her eyes.

They walked and walked until finally Mimi saw a restaurant and said, "Hey, here's a place to eat. Let's go inside and get a bite." Papa held open the heavy wooden door while the weary travelers ventured inside.

The hostess sat them in a booth by the window with a view of the parking lot.

"Boy, this isn't really what I thought Alaska would look like." Grant said, his head hung low.

"Oh, just you wait, Grant" Mimi assured him. "Anchorage is a city, just like any other big city in the United States. We'll see our fair share of glaciers and mountains, just be patient."

"Even I knew that," Christina said under her breath to Grant, so her grandparents couldn't hear. Grant kicked her foot under the table.

"Hey kiddos, let's all fight nice," Mimi said.

The waitress approached the table and asked with a cheery smile, "So, will you folks be having our Gold Dust soup this evening?"

"Wow! What's that?" Grant asked, forgetting his usual shyness around strangers.

"Haven't you heard that gold rush story?" the waitress asked, then continued when they all shook their heads. "Well, back in the days of the Gold Rush that started in 1872, it has been said that a restaurant owner earned more money than most of the prospectors by serving his Gold Dust Soup."

"What's a prospector?" Grant asked.

"Those were the folks who came in hopes of discovering gold," Mimi said

"That's right," said the waitress. "Anyway, the restaurant owner kept a pot of soup boiling on the stove," she continued, "And each time a prospector would pay for his dinner with gold dust, the restaurant owner would measure the dust with his greasy spoon and rinse it off in the soup. By the end of the season, a great deal of gold dust had settled to the bottom of the soup pot and the restaurant owner closed up his restaurant and headed back to the 'Lower 48'—much richer than many of the prospectors!"

Papa smiled, "That's a great story. But, I think I'll stick with a good ol' fashioned steak."

Delighted, Grant said, "I'll have the Gold Dust soup, please," and spent the rest of the meal studying each spoonful of the seemingly ordinary vegetable soup before slurping it down.

"Mimi, when are you going to go meet with the musher?" Christina asked between bites.

"Well, I thought we'd spend some time looking around Anchorage and then we'll head out to Wasilla to the dog sled training camp to take a ride on the Iditarod dog sleds. That's where I'm supposed to meet up with Mr. Joe Rutledge, the musher."

"I can't wait!" Grant said.

"Are you sure you don't need me to come along and help you on the Iditarod Trail, Mimi?" Christina pleaded.

"Hey, that's not fair!" Grant wailed.

"Trust me, you two. If this trip ends up like any of our past trips, you'll end up with plenty of adventure on your own," Mimi said.

"What is the Iditarod, anyway?" Grant asked. "I mean, I know it's a dog sled race, but how did it ever get started?"

Before Mimi had a chance to answer, Christina interjected. "You remember Grant. It's just like that story, *Balto*, we read."

"Oh, you mean about the dog who saved the sick children?" asked Grant. Christina nodded her head. "That is one of my most favorite stories."

"Yes," Mimi said. "I think it was in 1925. A horrible virus called diphtheria hit the children of Nome and the town had to rely on dog sleds to travel from Anchorage to Nome with the antidotal serum to cure them."

"Dip-what-ee-ah-?" asked Grant.

"Dip-thee-ree-ah," said Mimi. "It's the 'D' in the DPT vaccine—the vaccination shot the doctor gave you when you were little."

"Oh," Grant said, vaguely remembering the ouchie sting of the shots at the doctor's office.

"How far is Nome from Anchorage, anyway?" asked Christina.

"I think it's just over one thousand miles." Papa strained to recall.

"One *thousand* miles!  One dog ran one thousand miles?" Grant shouted in disbelief.

"No," Papa said. "They had a bunch of dogs and stopped at different check points and passed the serum on to the next dog sled.  Sort of like when you ran that relay at school on field day."

"Oh, cool," Grant said, slurping his soup.

"Remember when we went to New York and saw Balto's statue in Central Park?" Christina reminded Grant ,as she dredged one of her last fries through a huge puddle of ketchup. "He was the lead dog that ran extra far and long, something like twenty hours without stopping," she said as she popped the fry in her mouth and wiped the ketchup dribble from her chin.

"It will be awesome to see where the story actually took place," Grant said, stifling a yawn.

Papa paid the tab, tipping the waitress extra for her fun personality and entertaining stories.  She smiled at him, then looked at Christina and said, "Be sure to go by the National Cemetery in Eklutna Village National Park before you leave town.  You may get to see some native ghosts searching for their long-lost gold."

Christina's stole a glance at Mimi who was standing and attempting to pick up a now sleeping Grant.

"Oh," Christina said, sighing. "Too bad my brother is already asleep. I wouldn't want him to miss all the fun. Maybe we can do that another time." She looked up at her Papa, hoping he would back her up.

"Yes, I think you're right, Christina," he said. "We may need to save that for another night. We all need to get some rest to be fresh for tomorrow."

Across the restaurant, sitting in a dark corner, the same moustached man that had followed them through the airport ducked behind his menu. He quickly threw some crumpled bills on the table, and waited a few minutes before tracing the steps of the four tired Georgia tourists back to the Gold Rush Hotel. What was he up to?

# 3
# GLACIERS GALORE!

The next morning, Mimi woke the children with a surprise breakfast in bed.

"Room Service!" she exclaimed. She had ordered sourdough pancakes for Grant, and Christina's favorite, waffles. Mimi and Papa shared an omelet and toast and drank hot steaming mugs of coffee. Christina couldn't understand why they would ever choose yucky old eggs over sweet fluffy waffles. Adults could be so weird!

"Before we leave for the dog sled training camp, I thought it would be great fun to take you on a little day cruise so you could see the glaciers up close and personal!" Mimi said. "What do you think?"

"Yay! Yes! That sounds awesome!" Christina exclaimed, dripping syrup on her pink pajamas. "Oops."

Grant enthusiastically agreed, and they hurriedly finished their breakfast and dressed as quickly as they could, which was actually very slow, since they had so many layers to put on. Mimi told them that by dressing in layers, they would create pockets of air to help keep their bodies warm. They had to wear tight waffley shirts and pants called long underwear (the mere mention of the name sent Grant into fits of giggles), and turtlenecks, which Christina hated pulling over her head. After they put on gazillions of other clothes, they had to pull big snow boots over their pants, so the snow wouldn't slip down in their shoes and make their toes freeze.

By the time they all were finally fully dressed, they waddled out like ducks into the bright sunlight and cold breeze. Fine snowflakes floated from the sky like downy goose feathers, making Christina feel like she was inside one of those glass snow globes.

"Let's see who can catch the most snowflakes on their tongue," Christina challenged. They all joined her in sticking out their tongues and tilting their chins to the sky.

"I won!" exclaimed Grant.

"No way!" Christina said. "I got more than you, definitely."

Grant dropped to the ground and started flailing his arms and legs wildly.

"What are you *doing*, Grant?" Mimi asked.

"I'm making a snow angel," he said, as he swished through the snow.

Then the rest dropped to the ground and joined him, leaving their angel masterpieces on the sidewalks of Anchorage.

Finally Mimi said, "Let's go, guys! We've got glaciers to see!" She had booked a mini-cruise through Kenai Fjords National Park to see some glaciers.

The boat had indoor heated cabins, but outside, where Christina and Grant preferred to be, it was freezing cold. Even though the thermometer read thirty-six degrees, which is actually a few degrees above freezing–thirty-two degrees Fahrenheit–the wind made it feel much colder. That's what they mean by wind chill factor. Today, the wind chill factor was six degrees below freezing. *Brrr!*

Christina and Grant ran outside on the deck and then slipped back inside to warm up, only to head back out again. Papa and Mimi took turns going outside with them while the other would take long slow sips from a shared cup of hot chocolate.

Papa brought binoculars in hopes of seeing all kinds of wildlife. The brochure boasted Dall porpoises, eagles, sea lions and otters, and humpback and orca whales, but it ended up being too cold for wildlife. Christine and Grant were content to marvel at the glaciers. The captain took them close to the active tidewater glacier so they could hear it cracking and moaning like a squeaky old bed.

A tall man in a dark green hooded parka stood on the deck watching the shoreline. He'd turn every now and again, glancing in their direction. But Christina and Grant were too enthralled with the scenery around them to notice.

"Thank you so, so much, Mimi!" Christina exclaimed, as they walked down the plank from the boat, her eyes still stinging from the cold. "That was the coolest thing I ever saw in my life." And she meant it.

"Me, too," said Grant. "It was really cool and really *COLD*!"

"Well," Papa said. "I guess we can just turn around and go home then, Mimi. What do you think?"

"No way!" both kids screamed in unison.

"No way, is right," Mimi said. "We're off to pack up our stuff and head on to Wasilla to the dog sled training camp. Mush! On you, Huskies! Mush! Mush!"

# WILD FOR WASILLA

The next day they set out for the Wasilla dog sled training camp.

"Wow, look at all the big pine trees," Grant said peering out the window. "They look like the ones in Georgia, except dipped in vanilla ice cream."

Mimi laughed. "Actually, those are called Sitka spruce trees. They are Alaska's official state tree," she said.

"You sure know a lot about Alaska, Mimi," said Christina.

"That's because I had to do a lot of research for the book I'm writing," Mimi said. "Hey, we've got some time to kill on our way to Wasilla, why don't I share a bit of Alaska history with you two? Would you like that?"

"Yes, please," Christina urged, eager to know all she could about this foreign-feeling land.

"First, where are all the igloos?" Grant asked. "I thought most Eskimos lived in igloos."

"Well, actually, the native Alaskan people prefer to be called Inuit and, believe it or not, they live in houses very much like ours back in Georgia," Mimi corrected.

"In-you-it?" Grant repeated.

"Yes," Mimi answered. "Alaska's original inhabitants were the Inuit, Aleut, and Indian groups."

"Do you guys know how much the United States paid to purchase Alaska back in 1867?" asked Papa.

"A million trillion dollars?" Grant guessed.

"No—only two cents an acre. Can you believe that?" Papa told them. "Alaska didn't become an official state until 1959. It was the forty-ninth state. It's the largest U.S. state and is more than twice the size of Texas."

"Isn't Alaska where the highest point is in the world?" asked Christina, feeling proud that she knew some Alaskan trivia too.

"The highest point in *North America* is Mt. McKinley, towering 20,320 feet above sea level," Mimi said.

"Whoa. How do you remember all that stuff, Mimi?" Grant asked.

"Oh, I don't. By the time I start my next book it will all have fallen out of my left ear to make room for my next subject," Mimi said, giggling.

Christina got quiet, staring out the window at the huge mountains jutting up from the side of the road. "I think I need to take a little break from all this information, Mimi," she said.

"Me too. How 'bout I beat you at another game of Crazy Eights, Christina?" Grant challenged.

"Ha! *You* beat *me*? You're on!" Christina said.

Grant won five out of seven games before they turned into the drive of the dog camp. They looked up from their game and read the sign that hung from the arch over the driveway: RUTLEDGE DOG SLED TRAINING CAMP.

"This tournament won't be over until it's over," vowed Christina. "I *will* beat you fair and square, but it looks like we need to stop for now."

Grant snatched the cards, put them back in the box, and said, "You're on, sister."

"That's right, kids," said Papa. "We're here."

"I thought the Iditarod left from Anchorage, Mimi?" Christina asked, confused.

"Yes, well that's how it was originally, but they ended up moving the official start to Wasilla and just doing a **ceremonial** start in Anchorage," said Mimi. "Actually, I think the course follows two different routes on alternate years. This year it's the northern course."

Before Mimi could go into a more detailed explanation, the sound of barking dogs—a lot of barking dogs—drowned out her voice. Christina couldn't believe how loud they were, even with the doors closed. She peered out from the safety of the SUV to a big fenced lot filled with dogs and countless doghouses.

The snow around the dogs was mushy and dirty. Some dogs ran in circles, pulling at their chains, struggling to get free, like they couldn't wait to get back to pulling sleds. Others sat on top of their doghouses howling like wild wolves, while others lay sleeping in spite of the noise, snuggled up in the snow like it was a toasty blanket.

"Oh, my gosh!" Grant exclaimed. "Have you ever seen so many dogs in all your life?"

# 5

# DOGS, DOGS EVERYWHERE!

The kids followed their grandparents' lead and opened their doors. They stepped gingerly from their seats, the cold air blasting them in the face, their ears struggling to adjust to the dog-barking racket.

"Hi. My name is Raven." A slim dark-haired girl stepped up to greet them, her hand outstretched in the way Mimi had always encouraged Christina to greet people, but she still felt too embarrassed most times.

"Hello. You can call me Mimi, and this is my husband and grandchildren, Christina and Grant," Mimi said as she shook the girl's hand.

Christina tried not to stare at the girl, but her light blue eyes seemed to match almost identically with the eyes of the Siberian husky pup she held, making her appear not exactly all human, but pretty just the same. Christina had read about Siberian Huskies. They are the kind with the blue eyes.

"Well, welcome," said Raven. "I know my Dad, Joe Rutledge, is looking forward to meeting you and helping you with your book. Would you like to come meet him? He's back in the warehouse. I'll introduce you."

"Sure," Mimi said. "Actually, if you can just point me in the right direction, I'm sure I can find him if you wouldn't mind showing my grandchildren around the place."

"If you're sure you'll be all right," Raven said. Mimi nodded, gave Christina's shoulder a reassuring squeeze, and ventured off with Papa to meet up with Mr. Rutledge. Grant and Christina followed close behind Raven to where she laid the pup back in a bed with its mother and the rest of the litter.

"You can hold one if you'd like," Raven said to Christina and Grant. Grant was more than happy to let his older sister be the first to try. Christina bent down and carefully picked up a pup, being ever aware of the mother dog's wary gaze.

"Oh, he's so soft and sweet," Christina said, nuzzling her cheek into the puppy's fur.

"Yes, but not for long," Raven said. "Soon he'll be as lean and muscular as the rest of them."

"Yeah, now that you mention it," Grant said, "These dogs don't look like the Husky dogs you see in movies or on television."

Just then a voice came from behind them, tough, yet friendly. "That's because those dogs are just fluff and no guts."

"Hey, buddy," Raven said to the dark-haired boy. "Guys, this is my brother. He's pretty into his dogs." She offered it as an excuse for his gruffness.

He was obviously younger than his sister with the same dark coloring, except for his eyes. They were dark, almost black, like his hair.

"Hi," said Grant. "I'm Grant. I'm seven. How old are you?"

"Asujutilli. Uvanga Hunter. I'm seven, too," he offered, littering his greeting with his native tongue.

"Cool," Grant said.

"Cool," Hunter said.

"How old are you, Christina?" Raven asked.

"Nine, but I'm almost ten," she said, trying to appear older than her years. She assumed Raven was in her double digits, until she smiled, revealing two missing front teeth.

"I'm eleven," Raven said, her hands instinctively covering her mouth to hide the gaping hole where her two front teeth should be. "I know I look younger, because my teeth haven't come in," she said, embarrassed. "My Dad says I'm just a late bloomer."

Christina thought about the fact that she already had both her two permanent front teeth and was only nine. She'd never met a toothless eleven-year-old before.

Raven continued, "I don't really mind as long as they believe me when I'm fourteen and old enough to ride in the Junior Iditarod. I can't wait! I helped my cousin, Macy, train and get ready for last year's race. She didn't win, but she said it was lots of fun."

"Wow! I didn't even know they had one of those," Christina said. "Like an Iditarod for kids, right?"

"Yep. It's much shorter, of course. The Junior Iditarod runs about 160 miles, compared to the Iditarod which is 1,049 miles. It actually **fluctuates** each year, since they alternate the trails. But they say 1,049 miles to honor of Alaska, the 49th state," Raven explained. "Anyway, if we keep losing dogs the way we have been, I may never get the chance to race."

"What do you mean?" Christina asked. "There seems to be more than enough dogs here. It looks like at least a hundred," Christina said, looking at the dogs—too many to count.

"No. More like forty-five," Raven said. "But we've been trying to solve something quite puzzling around here lately. Seems some of our dogs have been coming up missing."

"What? Without a trace?" Grant asked.

"Yes. No footprints leading out of here. No nothing," Hunter said suspiciously. "My dad had to start sleeping out in the warehouse at night to make sure no more dogs disappeared."

"Yikes, that sounds too cold for me," Christina said. "My brother and I are actually pretty good at solving mysteries. We could help you, if you'd like?"

"That'd be great!" said Hunter. "Let's show you two around.

*But not all mysteries were so easy to solve.*

# 6
# THE MOST FANTASTIC NEWS!

Christina and Grant were just in time to help feed the dogs, which took over an hour, since they had to cart pound after pound of dog food from the warehouse where thousands more were stored.

They put the dog food into a big vat, then placed it on top of an ash-stained barrel that had wood burning in the bottom. When the food was thoroughly heated, they gave it to the ravenous dogs.

"P.U.!" said Grant, wrinkling up his nose as Hunter scooped the dog food into the bowls. "That stuff stinks! What's in it?"

"Oh, we go fishing every spring and catch salmon when they spawn and swim upstream," Hunter said. "Then, we mix the fish with the regular dog kibble. We freeze it and cook it up as we need it. The dogs need extra protein to build strong muscles and extra fat to keep them warm when they aren't as active. Their stomachs can actually take in twice as much food as they really need, allowing them to store up extra energy."

"Fish?" Grant asked, still plugging his nose. "Whole fish? Don't they choke on the bones?"

"Nope. Just watch," Hunter said. "When they're done eating, there'll be fish bones at the bottom of their bowls."

Grant watched while the dogs devoured their food and left piles of bones in their bowls when they were done, licking their fishy-smelling lips in contentment.

Grant helped Hunter pull the hose, weaving it around all the doghouses, and fill the buckets with water. First, they had to break the ice that had formed in the buckets. Grant raised his knee high and brought his foot down hard upon the ice's surface, shattering it into millions of pieces, which scattered across the snow like shards of broken glass. The dogs learned to drink the water quickly before it froze in the sub-freezing temperatures.

By the time the kids were done working, they were famished. Raven suggested they all go inside to warm up and get something to eat.

They opened the door to the kitchen and the smell of freshly-baked chocolate chip cookies wafted past their cold noses. Raven's mother, Sally Rutledge, welcomed them with a smile as warm as the fireplace-heated room.

"Asujutilli. Uvanga Mrs. Rutledge, Raven and Hunter's mom. How are you?" she asked.

"Uvanga Christina. I'm great," Christina said, trying out the new language. Christina could see where the kids got their fine looks, though Raven must have gotten her blue eyes from her Dad, because Mrs. Rutledge's eyes were dark like Hunter's.

"I'm co-o-o-o-ld," said Grant shaking.

"Well, come on in and get warmed up by the fire. I've got fresh cookies and hot chocolate if you'd like," she offered.

"Yum!" squealed Christina. Then she asked, "Mrs. Rutledge, are you Inuit?"

"Why yes I am, Christina," Mrs. Rutledge said, impressed by Christina's correct terminology. "You are a very bright girl. I can tell." Christina smiled.

The four children accepted the warm cookies and hot chocolate. They forgot about their cold toes as soon as the frothy marshmallow that topped the hot chocolate hit their tongues.

They laughed and shared stories about their friends, schools, and things that they most liked to do. Grant and Christina told them about all the different escapades they'd been on with Mimi and Papa. Hunter and Raven just stared open-mouthed in disbelief. As the words poured from Christina's lips, she realized that it was pretty hard to believe that they'd been to so many different places and had so many different fascinating experiences, especially at such a young age.

Just then, the door popped open and Mimi and Papa entered, followed by Mr. Rutledge. Christina was thankful for the distraction, but she couldn't wait to find out more about the missing dogs when the grown-ups weren't around.

"Hey, guys," Mimi said cheerfully. "Have you been having a good time?" she asked, knowing the answer just by the rosy-cheeked happy expressions on their faces.

"Awesome!" blurted Grant. "This place is the coolest place on the planet! Can we move to Alaska and raise sled dogs?"

"Uh . . . ," Papa said. "I think I can answer for your Mom and Dad on this one, pal. A big fat 'No.' But, you sure can enjoy the place while we're here."

"We have some pretty exciting news," Mimi said. "I think you'll be very pleased."

"What is it?" Christina asked. If Mimi thought something was exciting, then it had to be

# Mmmm. . . hot chocolate!

EXTREMELY exciting. Christina knew this from past experience.

"Well, I've talked to Mr. Rutledge and he has gotten special permission to have a second sled, so we can bring all you kids along on the Iditarod dog sled race!"

"Now wait just one minute," Mrs. Rutledge said. "Do you realize how cold it gets out there—how dangerous it can be?"

"Now, honey," Mr. Rutledge said. "We've talked it over and we think that if we split the kids up and have an adult on each sled, it will be safe enough." Mrs. Rutledge gave Mr. Rutledge a worried look, but pursed her lips to keep from saying anything more in front of the guests.

Christina's eyes went from Mimi to Papa, to Mr. Rutledge, and back to Mimi. "Are you kidding? Are you joking?" she asked in disbelief.

"No, no," Mimi assured her. "You know I wouldn't tell you something that wasn't true. We really think you guys can come. I mean it."

Grant and Christina, Raven and Hunter all jumped up from the table at the same time, knocking over chairs, and spilling hot chocolate all over the table.

"Yippee! Yippee!" they all yelled in unison, grabbing each other in one big group hug that included more jumping and turning in circles.

"I just can't believe it!" screeched Christina. "This is the best day—the most exciting—the most thrilling day of my whole entire life."

Little did Christina know that this was just the beginning.  Soon she'd be boot-deep in a mystery that could threaten the lives of her whole family, not to mention the Rutledge family.

# HOLD ON FOR YOUR LIFE

Raven and Hunter promised to take Christina and Grant on a dog sled ride, and they couldn't wait.

Raven wore a kusbuk. It was a parka, just like Christina's, except it didn't have a zipper. This supposedly made it warmer, plus she didn't have to worry about the zipper freezing up or breaking. She just slipped it over her head. Christina envied the color. She wished Mimi had gotten her a hot pink parka.

The Rutledges had many different sleds parked by the warehouse. Two small ones, sandwiched in between two large ones, looked just the right size for kids.

Before they went on a ride, though, they'd have to feed and water the dogs again. It seemed as though as soon as they finished caring for the dogs, it was almost time to start all over again, but Grant didn't mind. Though, he did start to rethink his idea of having his own dog sled training camp.

"Phew, this is a lot of work," Grant said, sweating under his parka.

"It sure is," Hunter said, "but, it's way worth it. These dogs are the best friends a guy could ever have." He unleashed a white dog named Bo, whose shoulders came up to Hunter's hip.

"Hey, there, pal," Hunter said, scratching a dog behind the ear. "Meet Grant, your new best friend," he said looking the dog in the eye. Then looking at Grant, said, "This Malamute is one of the most loyal dogs you'll ever have a chance to meet. You be good to him, and he'll follow you anywhere."

Hunter slipped Grant a dog biscuit and he in turn handed it over to Bo. From that point on, Bo and Grant were inseparable. Wherever Grant went, Bo was sure to follow.

"Hey, Bo-Bo, white as Snow-Snow," Grant said. The dog licked his face in a friendly response.

Raven announced, "Are you guys about ready to go for a real ride on the dog sleds? Get a little taste for the Iditarod?"

"Yay . . .yes!" Christina shouted. "Are we allowed to go by ourselves?"

"Yeah, my Dad has let us go on the trails around here. We've been sledding since we were toddlers," Raven said. "We usually race each other on the small sleds, but let's all jump on one, so we can be together."

"Sounds great!" Grant shouted.

Raven explained the sled to them and how to hitch up the dogs. She said, "The lead dog is in front. Behind him are the swing dogs. They help bring the other dogs into the turn. Then behind them are the team dogs and right in front of the sled are the wheel dogs. You can have from twelve to sixteen dogs in the Iditarod. We'll take sixteen. That way, if we need to, we can drop some if they get sick or injured."

"That sure is a lot of dogs," Christina said.

"Here, take these," Raven said to Grant and Christina handing them a bunch of socklike booties. "We have to put these on the dogs' feet to protect them from web cracking. That's what happens when dogs *don't* wear the booties, and snow and ice ball up inside their paw, causing sores."

"Once that happens, it's all over. The dog can't finish the race, so we have to be extra careful," Hunter said, his face stern, brows knit.

Raven hooked Bo's harness to the neckline, explaining to Grant that it would keep the dog from turning around and tangling the team.

Christina put a pair of pink booties on a female dog named Zaney. "Do you have pink booties so you can match your pink parka?" she asked.

Hunter snickered.

"No," Raven said. "Actually, the pink booties are just the easiest color to find in the snow."

"Oh," Christina said.

Hunter and Raven could outfit three dogs to each of Christina and Grant's one, but they all worked together to form a good team.

"Okay, I think we're set," said Raven. "We've got King at the lead, because he's both fast and intelligent. Then there's Zaney and Bo, our swing dogs. Behind them are Eli, Duchess, Kisses, Diva, Taz, Jules, and Misty," Raven announced. "Misty is the nutty one jumping up and down. She gets so excited, she can't sit still."

All the dogs seemed anxious. They pulled and pulled at the line, their excitement was contagious, making Christina want to pull and jump too.

Raven showed Christina and Grant where she would place her feet on the runners, which were the two bottom pieces of the sled covered with plastic that came in contact with the snow. She had them sit in the basket with Hunter.

"What's that bar called you're holding onto?" Grant asked.

"It's the handle bar," said Raven.

"Oh, just like on our bikes," Christina said.

"To stop the sled, you have to stomp on this brake pedal," Raven instructed. Christina was shocked that the mushers stood up the whole time they were driving the sleds. She couldn't imagine standing for over 1,000 miles.

"Each dog can pull a two hundred pound person and all they want to do is run, run, run. So, we need to be careful. It's very important to know how to use the brake to stop or it can be like being on a stagecoach with runaway horses," Raven said.

"Line out!" Raven shouted to the dogs, using the command to pull the team straight out from the sled.

Before Christina had a chance to get too nervous, she heard Raven belt out a loud, "Mush, Hike! All Right! Let's go!" and they were off! Christina and Grant grabbed extra tight to the sides of the basket.

"We're going about twenty-five miles an hour!" Raven shouted over the wind.

"Wow!" Grant exclaimed. "That's as fast as Mimi drives in the school zone. It feels a lot faster on a sled."

"Wa-hoo!" Christina shouted. "This is better than the roller coasters at Disney World!" The cold wind stole their breath and froze tears to their cheeks along with their smiles.

"All Right! Hike Up!" Raven yelled, instructing the dogs to go even faster. The sled zipped through the trails. Small branches brushed against their nylon parkas, making loud whooshing sounds. The rest of the kids cheered in delight.

"How do you turn this thing?" Christina asked. "Where's the steering wheel?"

"It doesn't have one," Raven said. "You turn it by leaning on the runners, sort of like downhill skiing."

After a while Christina began to feel comfortable with the speed and loosened her grip, soaking up the beautiful scenery around her. Snow-covered Sitka trees surrounded the trail, their branches almost touching overhead, making her feel like she was in a tunnel. In the distance, a mountain reached into the sky, hiding its peak in the billowy clouds.

Grant peered through the trees. "Raven?" he asked. "We aren't going to see any bears out here, are we?"

Before Raven had a chance to answer, Hunter belted out, "Nope. All the big grizzly bears are busy hibernating for the winter. They are fast asleep."

"Whew!" said Grant.

"We do need to be careful about moose, though," said Raven. "They can get pretty angry if a dog pulling a sled disrupts their peaceful surroundings."

"Hmmm," Grant said, not sure he wanted to mess with a moose.

Hunter took a handful of some kind of snack and popped it in his mouth. "Want some?" he said, offering Christina the bag.

It looked kind of strange, but Christina didn't want to seem rude, so she popped some in her mouth, too. She chewed it suspiciously, then asked, "What *is* this?"

"It's pemmican," Hunter said. "Dried meat mixed with berries and animal fat."

*Ugh!* Christina just smiled at him sweetly.

# 8

# MISSSING MALAMUTE

They rode and rode for what seemed like hours, but when Raven called, "Come Gee!" ordering the dogs to make a sharp right turn to head back to the camp, none of the children wanted the ride to end.

On the return trip, they rode by a frozen lake. They saw a man sitting on the ice, beside him a knee-high pile of dead fish. He held a fishing pole. Its line dangled into a small, round hole cut into the ice.

"That must be what they call ice fishing," Christina guessed.

When they finally returned, the dogs panted with exhaustion. The children were panting too. Their legs felt like Jell-O from standing and balancing on the runners. Raven had given them each a chance to stand on the runners to get a feel for being a real musher.

"That was a complete fantastico BLAST!" Grant shouted. "Can we go again?"

"Well, actually, believe it or not, we can," Raven said. "We just need to hitch up new dogs. We have some tourists scheduled to arrive in about an hour. We let them ride on the dogsleds and it helps to train the dogs and keeps them in good shape. Plus, the tourists pay us money for the ride and we use it to buy supplies and food for the dogs," Raven said. "It's a pretty good deal all around."

Hunter had walked to the back of the pen to tie up Misty. "What is going on?" they heard him shout. "Someone took a dog in broad daylight! Where's Dad?" he said, running towards the house.

"Wait a minute," Christina said. "Maybe there are some fresh footprints we can follow."

"I'll handle the tourists," Raven said. "Why don't you three start exploring until I get back?"

"Good idea," Grant said.

They spent an hour searching for clues around the camp.

"No footprints. No paw prints. No nothing," Grant said. "We better go tell the adults what has happened."

"The only footprints I saw, besides our smaller ones, were Mr. Ryan's, but his are all over the place," said Hunter.

"Who's Mr. Ryan?" Christina asked.

"He's my Dad's helper," Hunter said. "They're going to be partners in the Iditarod, and they've been friends forever. He does the best magic tricks. Wait till you meet him. You'll really like him."

As if on cue, a tall dark haired man came walking out of the warehouse. "Hey, guys. What you been up to?" he asked.

Hunter introduced him to Grant and Christina and then told him about the missing dog. "This isn't another one of your magic tricks, is it Mr. Ryan?" Hunter asked.

"No, Hunter. I'd never do something like that," Mr. Ryan said. "But who would?" He reached for Hunter's ear, pulled out a quarter and handed it to him.

Grant and Christina gasped.

"How do you *do* that?" Hunter said, forgetting the missing dog.

"I'll never tell!" Mr. Ryan said. "I'll see you kids later. And I'll keep my eyes peeled for any missing pups."

"Did you guys find anything?" Raven asked, returning from her ride with the tourists.

"Just a magic quarter," Hunter said.

The kids headed up to the house in search of the adults. They never noticed the narrowed eyes scowling at them from behind the nearby Sitka branches.

"Phew, that was close. Those kids almost came back too soon and caught me red-handed," the man said under his breath. He twirled his moustache between his forefinger and thumb. "I'll have to think of something new to keep the Rutledges and their friends from winning the Iditarod."

# 9
# SOURDOUGH AND
# SICK DOGS

The next few days went along smoothly. No more stolen dogs. Christina and Grant felt like experienced mushers, born to train for the Iditarod. They took turns mushing, having races against one another on the small sleds—girls against the boys. No one could agree who won.

Friday morning, they woke as usual and enjoyed another one of Mrs. Rutledge's hearty breakfasts. She made sourdough pancakes from scratch and served them with real maple syrup, bacon, and hot chocolate.

"These pancakes are even better than the ones that I had at the Gold Rush Hotel," Grant said.

"Qujannamiik," Mrs. Rutledge said.

"Except, I don't get to eat them in bed," Grant grumbled.

"Nobody gets that kind of special treatment around here, Grant. No matter how much we like you," Mrs. Rutledge teased. "I bet you don't know what makes my sourdough pancakes so good," Mrs. Rutledge said, getting blank stares in return. "I make them from a sourdough starter that was handed down to me from my grandmother who got it from her mother."

"What's a sourdough starter?" Grant asked.

"It's a blend of microscopic fungi living in a friendly environment of flour and liquid. Whenever I use some of it for my recipes, I just replace that amount with equal parts of flour and water and it keeps the starter **replenished** for the next time."

"Yuck," Grant said, before he had time to think about being polite. "We ate *fungus*? Isn't that moldy green stuff?"

"Not in this case," Mrs. Rutledge said. "It just helps the flour to rise. This particular batch is a blend of two starters. One that came from an old Alaskan gold prospector and one that crossed the American prairies in a covered wagon, combined to make one special batch. My ancestors have kept this batch going for over one hundred and fifty hundred years!"

"Wow," said Christina. She'd never heard of such a thing. Mimi always made pancakes from the boxes of mix she bought at the grocery store. *Just add milk.*

"Didn't they call prospectors Sourdoughs?" Mimi asked.

"Yes," Mrs. Rutledge said. "Most likely, because that was often the only food they had to eat in the mining camps and on their journey to find gold."

Mr. Rutledge broke in from the head of the table, "Okay, troops, enough sourdough history. Let's start thinking about the race. Today is the day. We need to finalize all our supplies for the race. Raven, I need you to check the food rations and make sure we have enough booties for all the dogs. Tomorrow we head out on the Iditarod Trail!"

"Oh, how exciting!" Christina said. "I can't wait!"

"What about water?" Grant asked.

"We don't need to bring water, Grant," Mr. Rutledge explained. "We'll just melt snow when we get to each checkpoint."

"Oh, yeah. That makes sense," Grant said, blood rushing to his cheeks like a winning lead dog.

"Don't worry about it," Christina said to him quietly. "I was wondering the same thing." They traded smiles.

Suddenly, Mr. Ryan stormed through the front door, startling everyone. Forks dropped, clanking on the heavy syrupy ceramic plates.

"Joe," he said. "We've got some sick dogs out here. You better come quick!"

Everyone dressed as fast as they could and headed out to the dog pens.

Six dogs were lying listless and panting on their sides. Their groaning sounded horrible—like a band of children attempting to play out-of-tune musical instruments without lessons.

The other dogs seemed to know that something was wrong. They didn't carry on and bark as they usually did when people came into the pen. It was like though they knew their dog pals were in trouble and they were quietly waiting for the humans to help.

"Poor, poor things," Raven cried. The sight of her beloved dogs lying so still troubled her terribly.

"It's going to be okay, honey," Mrs. Rutledge said, wrapping a comforting arm around her daughter's shoulder.

"Hurry, Ryan, call Doc Kemp, the veterinarian," Mr. Rutledge ordered. "We need his help–and fast!" Mr. Ryan obediently ran towards the house.

"Look at those blue drops of liquid around the dog's water bowls," Mr. Rutledge said. "If I didn't know any better, I'd think it was anti-freeze. It doesn't take much of that stuff to kill a dog," he added angrily, shocked by the thought that someone might have poisoned his dogs.

The children flinched in fear.

"That would mean that this was intentional–someone did this on purpose," Mr. Rutledge said. "I just can't imagine someone hurting poor innocent creatures. *Why?*" He asked the question more to himself than anyone else.

"It's the same creep who's been taking our dogs, Dad, I just know it!" Hunter said. "Someone is trying to sabotage us. Don't you see? These six dogs are our fastest, besides the one that came up missing the other day. Someone doesn't want us to win the Iditarod."

Christina struggled to understand and asked, "Who would do such a terrible thing?"

"Well, we can try to figure all that out later," Mr. Rutledge said. "Right now, we have to see if we can save these dogs."

"Oh, no!" cried Grant. "Not Bo!" He ran over to one of the sick dogs, got down on his knees and put his cheek against the fury animal's face. He looked up at Mimi. "Mimi. It's Bo. It's my friend, Bo. He's sick, Mimi." Tears poured from Grant's eyes.

Mimi ran over to Grant, scooping him up in her arms. He was much heavier now that he was pushing second grade, no longer the baby she remembered carrying so easily. "It's going to be okay, Grant," Mimi said. "Mr. Rutledge is going to get these dogs some help. Why don't we go inside and get out of their way?"

"No!" Grant shouted firmly. "I can't leave him. I won't leave Bo."

"Okay, okay, buddy," said Papa. "We'll stay right here beside him until the vet gets here. Don't worry."

But Papa looked *very* worried.

The vet is on the way. . .

# 10

# SIGH OF RELIEF

After what seemed like hours, but was truly only a few minutes, a black Hummer barreled up the driveway, crunching ice in its wake. A squat, balding man dressed all in black jumped out of the vehicle and rushed to the dog pen. He carried a black medical bag.

"What do we have here?" asked the man, who Christina figured was Doc Kemp.

"I think someone has poisoned my dogs, Doc," Mr. Rutledge said.

"I hate to say it, but I think you may be right, Joe," Doc Kemp said. "Why don't you have the children go inside and you and I and Ryan can get a good look at these dogs."

Despite the children's attempts to stay and help, Mimi and Mrs. Rutledge convinced them to go inside out of the cold. Mr. Rutledge promised Grant that they would help Bo first.

Grant grudgingly went inside, wiping his teary and dirt-smudged face with the back of his hand.

Inside the warm house, the children pressed their noses against the cold glass of the windows, their breath making foggy frost on the windowpane. They were all frustrated that they couldn't help, but Mrs. Rutledge and Mimi did their best to distract them with more cookies and hot chocolate. Christina had never had so much hot chocolate in her life!

"Hey, guys. Why don't we play a game of Junior Monopoly while we wait?" Raven suggested.

Before she could stop herself, Christina shouted, "Yes! I love Junior Monopoly. I call the blue car!"

It was the quietest game of Monopoly that Christina and Grant had ever played. Actually, by the time Mr. Rutledge came inside, they had played six games. That's a *lot* of Monopoly.

The door opened and Mr. Rutledge walked in, his head hung low, his eyes not meeting the children's anxious gaze. They could hear the Hummer retreating down the drive.

Raven ran to the door to greet her father, "What happened? Did Doc Kemp save the dogs?" she asked.

"Well," Mr. Rutledge said. "The good news is that we got to them soon enough and they were saved. Doc Kemp had to pump their stomachs and give them some medicine. We'll just have to wait and see if they can regain enough strength at this point to endure the race. It's tough enough when they're in prime condition. I just don't have very high expectations."

Grant's voice quivered as he asked, "What about . . . What about. . . Bo?"

Papa said, "Now, Grant. Don't you worry. Bo, actually, all the dogs, are going to be just fine—in time."

"But," Mr. Rutledge said, "I don't think in *enough* time to race tomorrow."

"We HAVE to ride in the Iditarod! If we don't, our whole trip out here will be a waste," Christina said, without thinking. "I mean. . . well, what I mean is. . . Mimi won't be able to write her book."

"I don't understand," Grant said. "There's like a million dogs out there. Why can't we use them instead?"

"That's a good question," said Mr. Rutledge. "I know that seems like it would make sense, but it all has to do with training. The six sick dogs are the strongest and smartest dogs, including the two lead dogs for both sleds. Yes, we have other dogs, but they aren't trained to run the sleds on a course as tough as the Iditarod," Mr. Rutledge explained. "That's why it's very suspicious that whoever poisoned the dogs seemed to know the exact dogs we had been training."

Mr. Ryan had stepped inside with the rest of the men, but now was making his way back to the door.

"Joe," Mr. Ryan said, "I'm going to go back out and check on the dogs. We'll keep 'em warm in the warehouse, until they're doing better."

Guess now wasn't the time to ask Mr. Ryan to do one of his magic tricks, Christina thought. She loved going to the local bookstore in Peachtree City when the magician would come to the children's section and do tricks for all the kids.

"Thanks, Ryan," Mr. Rutledge said. After Mr. Ryan left, closing the door behind him, he said, "Ryan is a loyal friend."

That night, the Rutledges prepared for the Iditarod as though their dogs were healthy. That way, they would be all ready to take off at a moment's notice if the vet deemed the dogs well enough to make the race. That was a BIG *IF*!

# 11

# GOOD NEWS!
# (AND NOT-SO-GOOD NEWS)

It was Saturday, the start day for the Iditarod! Raven and Hunter woke early, before the sun broke over the horizon and met up with their Dad, who had spent the night with the sick dogs in the warehouse.

Hearing their excited voices, Mimi, Papa, and Christina trickled out one by one to the dog pens to see what all the commotion was about.

King was perched high on top of his doghouse like a real king sitting upon his throne, feisty and strong. He appeared to be talking to the other dogs in low grumbling grunts and growls like an experienced football coach preparing his team for the Super Bowl.

The other dogs were all standing, and appeared to be healthy and eager to race. Misty had resumed her signature jumping and Zaney yipped in anticipation.

Grant was the last to step from the front porch steps and walk into the pen.

"Yay!" shouted Grant. "The dogs look great!

"Not so fast, Grant," said Mr. Rutledge. "I've got Doc Kemp coming out to check them over. We need to make sure King and Duchess are especially healthy, since they are the two team leaders."

The black Hummer crunched down the drive. The harried veterinarian hopped out and examined the dogs, one by one.

Everyone held their breath, waiting for the verdict.

Finally, Doc looked up and said, "I can't believe it! If you told me yesterday that any of these dogs would be able to run in the Iditarod, I would have told you that you were crazy. But, I've examined them all tip to tail and I'm here to tell you I really think they're all healthy enough to make it!"

"It's their spirit," Raven said. "These dogs want to win as much as we do."

Everyone cheered, and Mr. Rutledge hurriedly assigned each person a specific job to get ready as quickly as possible for the race. Grant was assigned the task of checking on the food and supplies for the first leg of the trip. As he turned to go into the warehouse, his eyes rested on an empty doghouse. It was Bo's.

"Where's Bo?" Grant asked. His heart raced as he saw the expression on Mr. Rutledge's face. "Where is he?" Grant asked again, searching Mr. Rutledge's eyes.

"I have no idea," Mr. Rutledge said. "I hadn't noticed he was even missing, to tell you the truth."

"He's gone. Bo's gone," said Hunter. "Don't tell me we've had another dog-napping on the start day of the Iditarod!"

After much emotional discussion, it was decided that Chloe would replace Bo. Unfortunately, they just didn't have time to find Bo, or any of the missing dogs for that matter.

"The race starts at 10:00 a.m. in Anchorage and that's a forty-minute drive," said Mr. Rutledge. "We don't have a second to spare."

"Hang in there, Grant," Papa said, as he squeezed Grant's slumping shoulder. "We'll get to the bottom of this and find your furry friend as soon as the race is over."

# 12

# BUSY, BUSY, BUSY

Last night, Christina had convinced Raven and Hunter that they needed to pull Mr. Ryan aside and see if he could help solve the mystery of the stolen dogs. But, everything had gotten so chaotic that by the time they set out to speak with Mr. Ryan, they couldn't find him. Now, that Bo was missing too, it seemed even more important to get Mr. Ryan on their side to help solve the mystery.

"Where's Mr. Ryan?" Raven asked her Dad.

"You won't believe it," he said. "Mr. Ryan got a wonderful opportunity to ride along with a friend of his in the race. I'll miss him, but I'm happy for him. It'll just mean that I'll need more help from Mimi."

"No problem," Mimi said.

"Wow! That's weird," Raven said.

"Well, I've got more to worry about right now than Ryan," said Mr. Rutledge. "I've got to get two sleds ready and all these dogs loaded, so let's go. Pitch in and help."

The kids helped load the dogs, thirty-two in all, into the trucks. Each team could have a maximum of sixteen dogs, according to the official Iditarod rules. Sixteen plus sixteen is thirty-two, Christina checked her math. Then, she looked at the trucks and laughed out loud.

"What's so funny?" asked Mr. Rutledge.

"Oh, it's just funny how the dogs each have their own special compartment. It makes me think of a dog hotel," said Christina.

"Hey, I never thought of it that way," said Mr. Rutledge.

The other truck carried the two sleds and supplies for the next couple days, including extra arctic parkas, heavy duty sleeping bags, an ax, snowshoes, musher food, dog food, and at least two pairs of booties for each dog's feet. They also packed a stove and water pot for melting snow and heating up the food, plus a first-aid kit and a vet log.

"What's this?" asked Christina as she helped pack.

"It's a ceremonial packet of mail," said Mr. Rutledge. "The Iditarod Trail was originally an old U.S. Postal route. Now teams carry cachets of mail that are postmarked in Anchorage and then cancel-postmarked in Nome. They can be sold as collector's items and can sell for several hundred dollars."

"Too cool," said Grant.

The rest of the supplies had already been shipped out to the many checkpoints between Wasilla and the Burled Arch–the finish line in Nome.

"Okay, guys! Is everyone ready?" asked Mr. Rutledge.

"Everyone be sure to go potty," Mrs. Rutledge warned like a veteran Mom. "Remember Anchorage is forty miles from Wasilla, and Mr. Rutledge *won't* be stopping on the way."

The four children made a beeline for the house, while the adults said their farewells.

They would be back home that evening. The start in Anchorage was just a twenty-two mile run to commemorate the original start. They would pack up the dogs, bring them home, and start all over again from the official start in Wasilla the next morning.

Mrs. Rutledge would stay back at the house to take care of the remaining dogs. She hugged everyone and promised to cook a nice warm meal for when they returned from Anchorage that evening.

The truck engines roared, the dogs barked, and they were on their way!

# 13

# ANCHORAGE AHOY!

The two rusty rattletrap trucks pulled into Anchorage.  Mr. Rutledge ran to the registration desk, while everyone else began releasing the dogs from the truck to get them harnessed and attached to their rigs.

"All set!" Mr. Rutledge said.  "I've got everyone registered and our postal cachet's stamped."  He walked around and checked and rechecked to make sure that each dog was properly rigged and all the supplies were secured.

"Let's make sure that all the dogs have their booties on," he said, tossing each of the kids and Mimi a bunch of booties.

Mimi fumbled around trying to get just one booty on Misty.  She couldn't get the antsy dog to sit still long enough to get the thing on her paw.  "This is worse than putting pantyhose on a pachyderm," Mimi complained.

Christina stepped over, after getting four of the dogs booted, gently took the booties from Mimi, and swiftly put them on Misty's four paws in less than a minute, then moved on to the next dog. Mimi stood back in awe, smiling proudly at her granddaughter.

"Okay," said Mr. Rutledge. "There will be an adult on each sled. I'll be on one with Mimi, Hunter and Grant. It goes against my better judgment to let you mush the other sled all by yourself, Raven, but without Ryan, I don't have a choice. I'll have Papa and Christina go with you. Do you think you can handle it?" he asked his daughter.

Raven fought hard to hide her enthusiasm. Christina could tell she was about to burst.

"Yes, Dad, I think I'll be fine," Raven said as calmly as she could, raising her brows and sneaking a smile at Christina.

"You girls better make sure that every inch of your bodies are covered, even your faces," Papa warned. He threw each girl a hat. "Put these on under your hoods. They pull down over your face like a mask. That way your noses won't get frostbite."

"Frostbite?" Christina asked.

"Yes, your skin can actually freeze if you don't protect it," Papa said. "Ice crystals can form inside your nose, for example, and damage the cells. If it goes on for too long, the tissue in your nose would actually die, turn black, and we'd have to have the doctor cut it off to save your life!"

"Gross, Papa!" Christina said.

"Yes. Gross. So, wear the ski mask," Papa said.

"Yes, sir," Christina said, pulling the mask over her face. "When can we take off?"

"As soon as Mr. Rutledge comes back and shows us where to line up," Papa said.

Christina was so excited that she thought her heart was going to tumble out onto the snow.

Momentarily, Mr. Rutledge returned. He had a strained expression on his face.

"What's wrong, Daddy?" asked Raven.

"Oh, nothing," Mr. Rutledge said. "Nothing, really, I suppose. It's just that I ran into Ryan over there by the supply tent and he's actually mushing his own team of dogs. Turns out his friend had some kind of family emergency and couldn't race, so now Ryan has taken his place. He's got a fine-looking team of dogs. Twelve in all, in fact."

"Wow! That's kind of odd, isn't it?" Raven asked. "Pretty exciting for him, huh? I wonder if he'd get to keep the whole prize if he ended up winning the race?"

"Guess he'd be as qualified as any to win the money. Whoever comes in first gets the prize," Mr. Rutledge said.

"What is the prize, anyway?" Christina asked Raven as soon as Mr. Rutledge walked over to the other sled.

"It's more than fifty thousand dollars!" said Raven.

"FIFTY THOUSAND DOLLARS!" Christina shouted. "I had no idea," she said more quietly. "That's more than a lot of adults make working a full-time job for a whole year!"

"Yes!" Raven said. "We'll be lucky to get the buckle."

"What do you mean?" asked Grant.

"Everyone who finishes the race gets a bronze belt buckle that says the year and *Iditarod Finisher*," Raven explained.

"How awesome!" Christina said. Now, *that* would be something to bring to school for show-and-tell. Too bad they stopped doing that in kindergarten.

Within minutes the race was on. There must have been sixty teams taking off in intervals from the intersection of 14<sup>th</sup> and D streets.  A huge banner hung over the street, billowing in the wind.

Raven situated her dogs directly behind her father's team where he instructed her to stay.  This was not a race that she would strive to win, at least not this year, she had told Christina.  Mr. Rutledge stressed to her the importance of staying with him during the race, as the weather and conditions could prove treacherous.

"Mush!  Hike!"  Mr. Rutledge shouted at his dogs.

"Mush!  Hike!"  Raven shouted at her dogs.

Christina held on tightly as the sled jolted from the starting spot and skittered over the rough snow.  The dogs were finally able to run freely, though the mushers held them back just a bit, so they wouldn't tire too quickly.  It was essential to pace them.

The wind stung their cheeks, even through the masks Papa had given them.  Christina was glad for the goggles Mrs. Rutledge had let her borrow, just before they left.  It helped keep her eyes from watering from the cold.

Papa yipped and yelled with excitement.  Christina had forgotten this was actually his first time on the sled.  She had been riding for days now, so the sheer thrill of riding wasn't as intense, but she sure was getting a taste for the musher's desire to win the race—it was infectious.

Grant waved wildly at Christina, and she waved wildly back at him, yelling, "Isn't this awesome?"

Grant smiled back at her and gave her the thumbs-up sign.

# GOLD-GONE

As Raven, Christina, and Papa came safely into Eagle River, Mr. Rutledge, Mimi, Grant, and Hunter were already off their sled chatting with excitement.

"Hey, there!" Raven said to the group. "Wasn't that fun?"

"Yes, and you did wonderfully. I'm very proud of you," Mr. Rutledge said.

"Gee, thanks, Dad!" Raven said.

"We came in second!" Grant squealed.

"Wow! That makes us third. Who came in first?" Raven asked.

Mr. Rutledge hesitated.

"Ryan! Ryan came in first!" blurted Hunter. "Can you believe that guy?"

Just then, a loud hullabaloo arose from the crowd that had gathered to watch the event.

"What's going on?" Mr. Rutledge asked one of the passing mushers.

"Well, you know the bars of gold they displayed in a glass case at the opening ceremony back in Anchorage?" the musher asked. Mr. Rutledge nodded.

"Evidently, they have been stolen!" the musher reported.

"Stolen?" Mr. Rutledge said.

"What gold?" Christina said. "I didn't see any gold."

"You must have missed that," said Mr. Rutledge. "You were so busy with the dogs, and we were in a rush. They had a display by the registration desk with bars of solid gold in the equivalent value of the $50,000 winning prize. It was just for show, but now it's gone."

"Who could possibly steal bars of gold right out from under people's noses?" Christina asked. "They'd have to be some kind of magician," she said. The mysteries just kept piling up.

The mystery of the missing dogs, the mystery of the poisoned dogs, and now the mystery of the missing gold. This was more miserable mushing mystery than even Christina could

# We can't believe it!

imagine! Christina would have loved to investigate, but they had to get back to Wasilla to get ready for tomorrow's race.

"I still don't understand why we have to start all over," Grant said, confused.

"Well, there is often not enough snow on this opening stretch of the race course," said Mr. Rutledge. "And a lot of times they end up with open water on the Knik River, which can make for extremely dangerous travel. After a number of accidents, the race commission finally decided to move the official start to Wasilla."

"Fine with me," said Papa. "I'll be happy to spend one last night in a warm, toasty bed."

Christina walked to the other truck to look for her missing mitten. She found it. She'd left it on the bumper when she pulled it off to close the compartments. As she pulled it back on her hand and walked around the rear of the truck, she plowed right into a hooded man wearing mirrored sunglasses.

"Oh, I'm so sorry," Christina said, startled.

"No problem, Christina," he said, as he took off his glasses. Christina realized then that it was Mr. Ryan.

She got the distinct impression that he was trying to hide something, when he said, "Pick a hand, any hand," tucking his hands behind his back.

Christina, caught off guard, tentatively pointed to his left hand.

A smiled brightened his dark face, revealing yellow stained teeth. He opened his gloved hand and extended it towards her, offering a small wood carving of a Husky dog.

"Take it," he said.

"Gee, thanks," she paused, feeling a bit uneasy. "Um, congratulations, Mr. Ryan. I heard you came in first,"

"Yeah, it's magic," he said. "See you tomorrow." To Christina, it sounded like a warning. He walked away carrying a duffel bag slung over his shoulder.

Wonder what's in there, Christina thought to herself as she noticed the shoulder strap cutting deep into Mr. Ryan's green parka. That must be one heavy bag.

Christina stole another glance at the wooden carving before heading back—only then noticing the wooden dog's sharp protruding fangs. Christina felt goosebumps pop up on her arms–and it wasn't from the cold.

# 15

# HAPPY TRAILS

After settling the dogs in for the night, the tired mushers enjoyed Mrs. Rutledge's delicious home-cooked meal of buffalo meat with Aalu—a dip made from choice parts of caribou. Then everyone snuggled in their cozy beds for one last good night's sleep before the long, grueling race.

That is, after Christina finally stopped her mind from racing with all the details of the ongoing and increasingly complicated mystery. She just couldn't believe gold could be stolen with security all around. She couldn't wait until morning when they'd get back on the trails and hopefully closer to solving some of the mysteries of this Arctic land.

After breakfast, the teams loaded up once again, and set out for the start, or RE-start of the Iditarod.

Now the *REAL* race will finally begin, thought Christina. No more messing around—from this point on, this was the real deal.

"You did such a great job of staying with us yesterday, Raven," said Mr. Rutledge. "I thought maybe Hunter and Grant could ride with you. That way, Papa could ride with the adults."

"Wow! That would be great!" the kids cheered in unison.

And so, they lined up for the great race. Although the crowds were cheering, Christina couldn't hear a thing, she was so bundled up and lost in her thoughts. And then–THEY WERE OFF!

As they sped off, Raven skillfully mushed her sled behind her father's, doing her best to keep up with his speed. The dogs seemed to be enjoying the ease of running through the *saluma roaq*, smooth snow.

"These are great conditions," Raven said. "Sometimes the snow can be really heavy and wet and hard for the dogs to pull through."

"We call that *natatgonaq*," Hunter said.

*Great* conditions? Christina thought. She'd never been so cold in her whole life! But, she couldn't remember the last time she'd had this much fun either. She knew she'd be sweating in the middle of a hot Georgia summer before long, so she decided to enjoy the moment. No matter *how* cold it was.

"Raven, I heard folks talking about rookies back at the start of the race. What's a rookie?" Christina asked.

"It's someone like me, I guess. It's a musher who is in the race for the first time or who has never completed the race," Raven said.

"I always thought a rookie was a baseball player who's new to the team," Grant said.

"That, too," Raven said. "It's sort of the same thing."

With plenty of time to chat out on the trail, Grant stole the opportunity to ask a question he'd been wondering about for quite a while.

"What does the word Iditarod mean, anyway?" Grant asked.

Raven strained to slow the dogs down a bit. Christina knew she was trying to keep them from exhausting themselves too quickly.

"The Athabascan Indians called their inland Haiditarod, 'the distant place,'" said Raven. "Later, when gold was discovered in the same area, miners founded the town at the Indians' hunting camp which they spelled, I-d-i-t-a-r-o-d and it stuck."

"I can see why they call it the distant place," Grant said. "After this, I'll surely keep my distance from any place under fifty degrees." He laughed, then grabbed tightly to the side of the basket. These trails were bumpier than a herd of camels.

They zipped by Knik, the Home of the 'Father of the Iditarod,' Joe Redington Sr., and the Mushers Hall of Fame.

Christina wished they could stop and look around, but she knew better than to ask. This racing thing was serious stuff.

After making quick stops at the first few checkpoints, Mr. Rutledge finally decided to stop for a longer break in Skwentna.

Papa and Mr. Rutledge built a small fire and melted snow in a tin pot to make water for the dogs. The boys and Christina took care of feeding the dogs, while Mimi opened cans of sardines and beans for the people to eat. If Christina was ever offered this food at home, she'd surely turn up her nose, but she was so tired and hungry, she couldn't even think about complaining.

They pulled out their sleeping bags. Mimi and Papa collapsed in the basket of one sled and Mr.

Rutledge laid in the other. The children preferred to curl up right beside the dogs that warmed themselves in the *api* (Inuktitut for 'snow on the ground').

Unlike the dogs, the children needed sleeping bags. They zipped their sleeping bags shut, leaving only a small hole to breathe out of and instantly fell asleep, only to be startled awake a few hours later.

The dogs barked as if to warn of impending danger. Christina unzipped her sleeping bag and jumped out. She spied another musher coming up the trail. He was so bundled up; she didn't recognize him, until he was almost past.

"Good morning, folks," said Mr. Ryan, as he flew swiftly by, kicking a fine dust of snow into Christina's eyes. "Hope you got a good rest. I'll see you at the finish," he said, followed by a low, grunting laugh.

Something glared into Christina's eyes. At first, she thought it was just the snow, but on second glance, she realized it was coming from a rip in Ryan's duffel bag—a reflection.

His dogs seemed to struggle with the weight of his sled. Christina couldn't imagine how his sled could weigh more than theirs, since they had more people. And yet, Mr. Ryan's dogs strained with each step.

"Christina, did you see that?" Grant asked.

"The bright light coming from that bag?" she asked.

"What bag?" Grant asked. "No. I meant the dog. That brown lead dog seemed really familiar. Did you see the way he watched me as he ran by? It's like he knew me." Grant said.

"No. Sorry. I didn't notice the dogs." Christina said rubbing her eyes and thinking they both must be seeing things.

# 16

# THE BIG BREAK

And so it went. The days poured by with much of the same. It felt to Christina like endless days of wind, cold, snow, and Cold, Cold, and more COLD! She got a glimpse of what it felt like to be one of those icy green popsicles that nobody wanted in the bottom of Mimi's freezer.

When Raven pulled their sled up next to Mr. Rutledge, Christina was thrilled to hear him say that they would be taking their mandatory twenty-four hour stop in Ruby, the next town, on the Yukon River.

When they pulled into Ruby, which appeared on the map to be about the halfway mark, everyone went about their duties of caring for the dogs and setting up camp.

Even though the temperature was below freezing, the wind had died down a bit, so Papa and Mr. Rutledge built a huge bonfire. Everyone gathered around with heaping plates full of smoked salmon and warm buttery mashed potatoes—they were the instant kind, but it all tasted gourmet to Christina, compared to what they'd been eating on the trail.

Mrs. Rutledge had the special foods delivered as a surprise. She attached a note written in Inuktitut, her native language.

Raven translated the note. "It says, 'I hope you are all staying safe and warm. I can't wait for your safe return,'" she read.

"You have the best Mom in the whole world," Christina said, appreciating the closest thing she'd had to a home-cooked meal in a long time.

"Don't let Mimi hear you say that, Christina," Grant teased. "She may tell Mom and then you'd never be allowed to go on another adventure mystery trip."

"Your secret's safe with me," Mimi said, enjoying the warm food just as much as Christina.

Afterwards, they sat around the warm fire, roasting marshmallows and making S'mores out of graham crackers and sweet milk chocolate. Now, this is good stuff, Christina thought, petting one of the dogs curled at her feet. Living life on the

Iditarod Trail sure can make a girl appreciate the small things in life.

Everyone sat quietly gazing into the campfire, reflecting back upon the last few days and thinking about what the next week would hold. Christina's mind wandered to—gold. She thought about the missing gold. And then she started thinking about the Gold Rush. She had heard about it when they studied history in school. It was hard to believe that she was actually sitting in Alaska where gold was once discovered.

"Mimi, did you learn about the Gold Rush when you were researching for your book?" Christina asked.

"Yes. Believe it or not, we are very close to where gold was discovered," Mimi said. "Actually, the *first* gold discovered on the west coast was in California, but fifty years later, in 1896, prospectors found gold here in the Yukon Territory."

"Given the choice, I would have been a California prospector where it's warm and toasty," said Christina.

"That's just it," said Mimi. "People didn't have the luxury of jumping on an airplane and panning for gold in California. It was much more difficult to get from place to place in those days, don't forget."

"How did they get the gold?" Grant asked, interested. His mouth was outlined in chocolate and short strings of marshmallow hung from his bottom lip like icicles.

"I know the answer to this one," Papa said proudly. "They *panned* for gold. They would use pans to scoop up dirt in the riverbeds and wash the dirt in the water."

"That's right," said Mr. Rutledge. "Gold is eight times heavier than dirt, so the gold would settle down to the bottom of the pan, and there they'd have it."

"Well, yes," Mimi said. "But they also mined for gold. They'd dig into the ground, sometimes as deep as 100 feet. A miner at the bottom of the hole would chip away at the dirt with a pick and put the dirt into a bucket that was attached to a rope. The miners standing up above ground would pull it up and wash it through a cradle."

"A cradle?" Hunter interrupted. "You mean like for a baby?"

"No," Mimi said, with an understanding smile. "A miner's cradle had a metal sieve that he'd

Nothing like a bonfire!

pour the dirt and water through while shaking the handle. The strained dirt and water would come out one end and the gold would settle in the bottom."

"That sounds like fun!" Grant said.

"Yeah, it probably was at first, but it was hard work and many prospectors came home empty-handed, not to mention all the crime that happened when folks got greedy," said Mr. Rutledge.

"Yes, I read that about 40,000 people reached the gold fields back then, but only about 4,000 found gold and only a few hundred struck it rich," said Mimi.

"Sometime, if you guys ever get back here in the summer, we'll have to take you to Skagway," said Mr. Rutledge. "It's a historic town that's been restored to look like it did back in the days of the Klondike Gold Rush. Nearby, is the grave of greedy 'Soapy' Smith, a notorious crime boss who was killed in a shootout."

"Wow!" said Grant. "That sounds like a tale from the Wild West."

The wind kicked up and the fire was burning out, so everyone decided to get a good night's sleep in the roadhouse. More like a road*room*. The quarters were tight in a room with five bunk beds. Grant and Christina flipped a quarter for the top and

Grant won.

As she was nodding off to sleep, Christina stole one last bleary-eyed peak out the frosty window by her bunk bed. Her eyes fell shut, but her mind kept racing like runaway sled dogs. Was that a shadow of a crouched man behind their sled or just a bag of supplies? Christina was just too exhausted to investigate. *Zzzzzzzzzzz.*

# 17

# RUNAWAY SLED

They headed out early the next morning with a quick breakfast of squaw candy and dried salmon berries. Today would prove easier on the dogs. They had just a bit more of uphill sledding before they started the descent to Nulato.

As they headed out on the trail they passed an exhibit of totem poles, which had been brought in for the race, that appeared to have weathered more winters than Papa. The large wooden poles jutted high into the sky. They were carved with various animal and bird faces, and some faces Christina couldn't quite decipher.

"What an amazing ancient art," Hunter said. "Someday I'm going to try to carve something like that."

Raven kept pace with her Dad's sled, but soon the wind picked up and with it, blowing snow—lots of it.

"The anniu is so thick I can barely see," said Hunter.

Within minutes, the kids were in the midst of a blizzard. They could hardly see a few feet ahead of them.

"Where are Mimi and Papa?" Christina asked in a quivering voice.

"I don't know," Raven said, trying her best to stay on what she could see of the trail. "I'm sure we'll catch up with them soon." She kept the dogs moving, and even though Christina couldn't see very well, she could feel that they were beginning to race downhill. The sled moved faster and faster, as the dogs rushed down the mountain.

"Raven? Shouldn't you slow down a bit?" Hunter asked.

"I'm trying to, but the brake doesn't seem to be working anymore," Raven said, as she stomped futilely on the brake.

"What do you mean not working? Didn't you check it before we left?" Hunter asked.

"I did check it, but something must have

come loose!" Raven said, stomping even harder.

The dogs ran faster and faster.

"Whoa! Whoa!" the children all screamed, but the dogs wouldn't stop.

"We could crash!" shouted Christina. "We could really get hurt." All the children started screaming even louder in a panic. "Whoa! Whoa!"

The snow came down harder and harder as though the clouds didn't have brakes either.

Christina squinted. She could have sworn she saw something red in the distance, like a spot of blood on a white blanket.

"Red!" Christina shouted. "It's them! It's Mimi and Papa! I can see Mimi's coat!"

Mr. Rutledge and Papa must have seen them coming, or heard their screams, more likely. At once, they surrounded the dogs, stopping the sled just before it plowed into theirs.

"What happened, Raven?" Mr. Rutledge shouted.

"The brakes went out," Raven said. "I can't figure it out. We checked and rechecked those things."

The memory of last night's crouched shadow hit Christina like a slap. She told them what she saw, convinced now that it really had been a man—

apparently tampering with the brakes.

"I just thought my eyes were playing tricks on me last night," she said. "I was so tired."

"Don't blame yourself, sweetheart," said Mimi.

"This time you should have trusted your instincts, Christina," Mr. Rutledge said. "Look down here. There are scratches on the brakes. It looks as if someone loosened them with a wrench. This is definitely a case of foul play. But who would do such a thing?"

This was no time to stop and talk. The wind and snow were treacherous. Christina shivered and her teeth chattered. She couldn't tell if it was her body's attempt to warm itself or just nervousness from the harrowing ordeal. She sure didn't want to get hypothermia—she could die from that!

Mr. Rutledge fixed the kids' sled, and they got back on the trail in search of Nulato.

# 18

# MOOSE ON THE LOOSE

They'd stopped for a quick catnap and dog check in Nalato and then got right back on the trail towards Kaltag. They'd been on the trail for a few hours when the snow finally trickled down to light flurries, but the wind still whistled through the trail like a runaway freight train.

Just before they reached the checkpoint, they saw something big and brown in the middle of the trail.

"Cool!  A moose!" cried Grant.

"Ah, how *cute*." Christina said, looking at the huge fuzzy antlers protruding from the big-nosed creature.

"Oh, no!" cried Raven.

"Uh, oh," Christina said, sensing Raven's concern.

Swiftly, like a seasoned musher, Raven stopped the dog team with a hearty, "Whoa!" This time, the brake worked perfectly.

"This is not good," Mr. Rutledge said. "Kids, stay back! Do not move."

Christina remembered Raven warning them about this very thing the other day when Grant was asking about grizzly bears.

"This is *not* cool," Grant decided.

The moose stood facing the dogs head-on and didn't look to be in any hurry to move or back down.

"Why do moose come down to the trail, Raven? Aren't they afraid of people?" Christina asked.

"It's much easier for them to walk on the trails that have been packed down by the snowmobiles and sleds, than to struggle through the deep snow," Raven said. "They can be quite vicious when it comes to getting their way and have been known to trample sled dogs and injure mushers."

"Yikes!" said Grant.

"Is that a pile of birch and willow branches on the trail?" Raven asked, more to herself than the other kids. "How would those have gotten there?"

"I don't know. Why?" asked Christina.

"That's what moose eat," Raven said.

Ahead of them, Mr. Rutledge donned his snowshoes.

"Everyone get down on the ground and cover your heads in case he attacks," he warned.

He grabbed the willow and birch branches and headed up the pass, attempting to coax the moose off the trail. At first the moose laid back his ears in defiance. Then the animal seemed to change his mind and followed Mr. Rutledge into the woods like a baby duck following its mother. Free food must have been more appealing to the moose than an easier walk.

Once Raven was satisfied that the moose was far enough away from the dogs, she yelled, "Mush!" moving the dogs up to Mimi and Papa's sled. Then she directed Papa on how to guide the dogs and they both moved the sleds up the trail safely away from the moose.

Mr. Rutledge laid the branches on the ground, then swiftly trekked through the snow back to the sleds, leaving the moose to munch his branches undisturbed.

"Excellent teamwork!" he shouted, as he returned.

"Yeah, but, Dad. . ." Raven said. "If I didn't know any better, I'd say someone put those branches there to deliberately lure a moose into our path. There's no way they could have gotten there all on their own in weather like this, especially in a nice neat pile. Someone set us up."

"Guess they didn't bank on us getting a *nice* moose," Christina said. There was only one set of sled tracks in the fresh snow. The culprit must already be on his way to Unalakleet, the next checkpoint.

# 19

# SAFETY SHOCK

They safely maneuvered through the towns of Unalakleet, Shaktoolik, Koyuk, Elim, Golovin, and White Mountain. As they pulled into Safety, the last stop before Nome, they saw Mr. Ryan's sled parked outside a small shanty, his dogs still hooked to the lines. The big shiny brown lead dog started barking wildly and pulling at the line, trying to leap frantically towards their sled.

"He wants to play," said Grant, as he got out of the sled and walked over to the dog. He knelt down to see if he could soothe him. As he looked into the dog's face, he was struck again with how familiar he looked.

The dog whimpered and snuggled Grant's chin.

"Hey, there, pup. How ya doing?" Grant said, extending his hand to pet the dog's head.

"Don't pet that dog!" A gruff voice demanded from behind Grant's back.

Grant spun around, shocked to see his own reflection in mirrored sunglasses. Mr. Ryan scowled at Grant, ice hanging from his dark moustache like a snotty nose.

"Oh, I'm sorry, Mr. Ryan," Grant apologized. "I didn't realize. . ." Grant didn't get a chance to finish his sentence.

"Well. . . " Mr. Ryan stammered. "I don't want my dogs distracted in this race. So, please. . . hands OFF!"

"Yes, sir," Grant said in the polite manner his parents had taught him to use when speaking to adults.

"So. . .you've caught up to me, huh?" Mr. Ryan said. "I had some trouble with a moose and it set me behind."

"So did we," Grant said, not sure whether to trust Mr. Ryan anymore. He didn't like it when adults spoke to him meanly. What kid did?

"Do you want to talk to Mr. Rutledge?" Grant asked. "He's right over there,." Grant pointed to the sleds. He started walking towards his grandparents, seeking their security.

"No," Mr. Ryan said curtly.

Grant noticed a dark brown smudge on the palm of his mitten.

"Yuck," he said out loud. "What's this? Dog poop?" He smelled his glove and recognized the scent. "This isn't poop! It's shoe polish!" he blurted. "Shoe polish," he repeated, suddenly understanding.

Grant shot Mr. Ryan a knowing look over his shoulder, then yelled, "Shoe polish! Shoe polish! That lead dog is covered in shoe polish!"

"What's going on, Grant?" Raven asked, turning from the line she'd been trying to untangle.

"It's Bo!" Grant yelled. "Mr. Ryan has Bo!" He jumped on Mr. Ryan's sled as it began moving out of the checkpoint. Grant pulled frantically at Mr. Ryan's parka.

Mr. Ryan pushed Grant and he fell off the sled, his head slamming hard on the icy snow.

"Back off, kid!" he yelled and threatened Grant with the axe he'd pulled from his supply bag. Mr. Ryan's eyes appeared glazed, as he looked at his own hand and lowered the axe.

"You better just back off!" he said more quietly.

Grant scrambled back on his elbows, getting as far away from Mr. Ryan as he could without turning his back on him.

"Mush! Mush!" yelled Mr. Ryan. "Let's go! I'm going to win this race, if it's the last thing I do. And nobody's gonna stop me!" He and his dogs were off—headed toward Nome—the finish line of the Iditarod Trail.

"Renegade musher!" yelled Grant struggling to his feet. "Renegade musher! It's Mr. Ryan!"

# THE HOME STRETCH

The other kids had been unloading their gear and hadn't yet unhooked the dogs. They jumped back on the sled, heaving the gear in as quickly as they could and were at Grant's side in under a minute.

"Jump on, Grant!" yelled Hunter.

Grant scrambled to his feet, and Hunter and Christina helped pull him into the basket.

"Mush! Hike!" Raven shouted to the dogs as their feet skidded on the ice. They swiftly pulled the sled onto the trail.

"Wait up!" Papa yelled after them. "Where are you kids going?"

"We're off to save Bo!" Grant shouted.

"And the gold," Christina yelled, realizing in that moment that Mr. Ryan must be the one who took all the dogs *and* the gold.

"Wait," said Mimi. "Wait for us!"

But it was too late. The kids were already far down the trail in pursuit of Mr. Ryan. Raven allowed the dogs to run at full throttle—no holding back! This was the home stretch of the race. They slowly gained on Mr. Ryan's sled, until the distance between them shrunk to only a few feet.

"Back OFF!" Mr. Ryan yelled over his shoulder.

"Not a chance!" Grant yelled back.

"You're a low-down dirty cheater!" yelled Hunter.

"Yeah, and cheaters never prosper," Christina echoed, not knowing why she said that, except to repeat what she'd heard Mimi say on the subject before.

"I've come too far to let some little whiney kids ruin this for me," Mr. Ryan threatened. "Come Haw!" he commanded his dogs to make a sharp left turn. The dogs obeyed, pulling the sled left and blocking the trail. "Whoa!" yelled Mr. Ryan.

"Come Gee!" yelled Raven. Her dogs veered to the right to avoid hitting Mr. Ryan's sled.

"Mush!" Mr. Ryan yelled at his dogs, ordering them to run again.

# He did it!

The kids' sled was stuck in a snow bank.

"Oh, no! He's getting away!" yelled Hunter.

Hunter, Grant, and Christina jumped out of the basket and pulled the sled out of the snowbank. Then, they all jumped back in and Raven yelled, "Mush!" They had lost precious time. Mr. Ryan was already well ahead of them on his way towards Nome.

"Mush, Huskies! Mush!" Raven commanded.

# 21

# FINISH LINE

The sky was black as they made their way down the twenty-two mile trail to Nome. With each passing mile, they had lost priceless hours of daylight.

The Aurora Borealis, better known as the Northern lights, danced in pastel-colored patterns across the sky.

As the dog sled glided towards the Burled Arch–the finish line in Nome, Christina noticed a red lantern hanging from the arch and asked Raven what it was for.

She explained that the lamp is called The Widow's Lantern and remains hanging from the arch until the last musher finishes the race, signifying the official end of the Iditarod for the year.

"Why a red lantern?" Christina asked.

"Back in the olden days when mail was delivered by dog sled, people used lanterns sort of like the way pilots use lights on a runway," said Raven. "It helped the mushers find their way through darkness and bad weather to deliver the mail to the roadhouses."

They came down the homestretch towards the finish line. The dogs scrambled and slid on the black ice, but regained their grip and Raven guided them skillfully over the finish line.

They could already see a race official putting the winning ribbon around Mr. Ryan's neck.

"STOP RIGHT THERE!" shouted Raven. 'That man is an imposter!"

Mr. Ryan looked over his shoulder in shock.

"You don't know what you're talking about! You're just kids!" he said. "I won this race fair and square."

"Oh, yeah," said Grant, jumping from his sled. "Then what's this?" He took a handkerchief from his pocket and wiped the shoe polish from the dog. The dog's coat changed from dark chocolate to pale gray, revealing a smudged Bo underneath. Grant unhooked the dog from the line and Bo licked his face in gratitude, bathing his cold cheeks in stinky, fishy dog breath.

"Bo!  You're okay!" Grant cheered, brown shoe polish on his nose.

The adults had finished right behind the kids. "Oh, that's wonderful," Mimi said, squeezing him in a hug.

Mr. Ryan tried to run, but Mr. Rutledge grabbed his sleeve, while Papa kicked his feet out from under him.

After Christina had realized that Mr. Ryan could not be trusted, she put the clues together in her head and figured out that he must have been the one who stole the gold.  He must have tricked the race security guards the same way he tricked the kids, with all his magic.

Christina ran over to Mr. Ryan's duffel bag and pulled it open forcefully.  The zipper broke and the bag gaped open revealing countless bars of glimmering gold.

"Ahhh!" a collective gasp arose from the crowd.

The missing and poisoned dogs, the missing gold, the suspicious brake, and the moose problem all led back to Mr. Ryan.  But why?

Mr. Rutledge looked Mr. Ryan in the eye.

"I thought we were friends, Ryan," he said, with glaring eyes.  "How could you betray me this way? What could possibly mean so much to you to do such horrible things?"

Tears leaked from Mr. Ryan's eyes as he pulled off the mirrored glasses.

"Joe, I know what a good musher you are," said Mr. Ryan. "You were really my only competition and I had to stop you. I know I messed up, but I *did* tell you about the sick dogs, before they got too bad," he said.

"You're the one that made them sick!" Mr. Rutledge snapped.

"I don't expect you to forgive me," Mr. Ryan said. "But this was bigger than friendship. This was family."

"What are you talking about?" Mr. Rutledge asked.

"My sister lives here in Nome," Mr. Ryan said. "She has cancer and no way to pay for treatment. I thought if I could cash in the gold and win the prize money from the Iditarod, I could help pay her medical bills."

"This sounds sort of like that Balto story," Grant said.

"Yeah, except in that story there was a hero, not a meanie villain," Christina said.

"Why didn't you tell me, Joe?" Mr. Rutledge said.

"I know you needed the money, too, after all you've invested," Mr. Ryan said. "And I know that winning the Iditarod is your dream. I realize now that I was wrong. Very wrong."

"Well, that doesn't excuse what you did," Mr. Rutledge said. "Even if your intentions were good for your sister, it doesn't mean you can harm other people, or dogs for that matter."

Mr. Rutledge and Papa continued to hold Mr. Ryan down until the police arrived. Then they clasped his wrists in handcuffs and escorted him back to the police station in Anchorage by helicopter.

"Wow!" shouted Grant, over the whirling sounds of the helicopter blades. "I'd love to ride in a helicopter."

"Not if it means going to jail," said Papa. "I'll give you a ride in *My Girl* when we get home."

"How are we going to get his dogs back home?" asked the race officials.

"Don't worry about those dogs," said Mr. Rutledge. "They aren't *his* dogs. They're *ours*!

# 22

# REINDEER STEW

Mr. Ryan was disqualified, and since the children weren't eligible to win, Mr. Rutledge took first place in the Iditarod. He grinned from ear to ear with pleasure. Since Mimi and Papa were his honorary partners, he offered to split the winner's purse with them.

"This experience and the material I've accumulated for my book is prize enough," said Mimi. "This has been a ride of a lifetime. We're all winners!" she said, hugging the children close.

After the last musher made it through the finish line, carrying the Widow's Lamp, the fireworks show erupted in the black sky with the Northern Lights as a backdrop.

Everyone celebrated by attending the Iditarod's traditional Reindeer Stew Potluck Dinner.

"Yummy," Christina said, as her fingers traced the engraving on her shiny bronze belt buckle.

Christina was so glad to be inside the warm roadhouse, she didn't even flinch at sampling the brown, musky meat stew. Like most kids, she never would have imagined eating reindeer before coming to Alaska, but after eating some of Mrs. Rutledge's ethnic Inuit dishes and the dried salmon and pemmican they ate on the Iditarod Trail, reindeer stew sounded quite delicious. And it was!

When it was time to pack up and say good-bye, all the children walked outside together.

Mimi decided to share one last bit of Alaska trivia. She said, "You know, I read that Nome supposedly got its name when someone who was charting the area didn't know what to call such a remote spot and wrote 'NAME?'. Later, a draftsman copied the word out as 'NOME,' and it stuck ever since."

"Ah," Papa said, with a twinkle in his eye. "There's no place like Nome!"

"I'll choose a long hot bath in Peachtree City over an icicle bath in Alaska, any day," Mimi said.

"Not me," said Christina. "I actually think I could learn to love the Land of the Midnight Sun."

"Me, too," said Grant. "I've learned to love all nine different kinds of snow. Snowpack, metamorphose, equitemperature, temperature-gradient, sugar snow, depth hoar, firnification, wet snow," he listed. "And, last but not least, spicules."

"Very impressive," said Christina. "Iditarod," she said softly. She just couldn't believe she had actually rode in–and finished–this famous race.

"I did a rod, too!" Grant insisted. "And I wish we could do it all over again! Right Bo?"

## Woof! Woof!

*Special thanks to our 'sled dogs.' We couldn't have done it without you!*

Kota, Malamute
*from New Hampshire*

Kody, Husky
*from Georgia*

Chippy, Husky
*from New Hampshire*

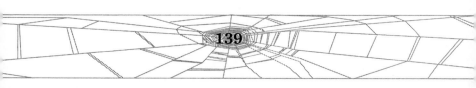

Now...go to

*www.carolemarshmysteries.com*
and...

- Add this book to your personal Adventure Map Tracker!

- Go on a Scavenger Hunt!

- Take a Pop(corn) Quiz!

- Hear from Mimi, Papa, Christina, and Grant!

- Talk to Christina and Grant!

- Join the Fan Club...and MUCH MORE!

# IDITAROD

- Dog mushing is the official state sport of Alaska, adopted by the legislature in 1972.
- The closest race finish occurred in 1978, when Dick Mackey crossed the line one second before Rick Swenson. The officials chose the winner based on the nose of the lead dog across the finish line.
- Since 1973, the Iditarod race has attracted 421 mushers from four continents and 15 countries (Austria, Australia, Canada, Czechoslovakia, England, France, Germany, Italy, Japan, Norway, Sweden, Scotland, Switzerland, Russia, and the United States) to compete.
- Folks have come up with several different meanings to the word "Iditarod" over the years, including "clear water" and "distant place."
- Today, the town of Iditarod is a ghost town.
- In 1994, Simon Kineen became the youngest musher to ever compete in the Iditarod. The oldest musher to ever compete is Colonel Norman Vaughn, 88, who raced five times.

# TRIVIA

- The term "musher" originates from the gold rushers who traveled to North Country in Alaska and fed their dogs mush.
- Dorothy G. Page is known as the "Mother of the Iditarod" because she helped organize fundraising to launch the first race.
- There are 26 checkpoints on the northern route and 27 checkpoints along the southern route.
- The Iditarod is the longest dogsled race in the world.
- Thousands of volunteers help organize the race, operate checkpoints, and support the mushers each year.
- Mushers often bring a small cooler along on the race, not to keep things cold but to keep food warm.
- Mushers celebrated the Iditarod's silver (25th) anniversary in 1997.
- Balto's dog partner was named Togo, a speed racer.

- The Iditarod Trail includes crossing over two mountain ranges and following the Yukon River for 150 miles.
- Mushers yell "Gee!" to make dogs turn right and "Haw!" to command a left turn.
- Film crews from England, Japan, the United States, Spain, and Germany have all covered the Iditarod event.
- Race winning times used to total as many as 20 days, but they have since shrunk to under 10 days.
- Though the Iditarod is officially 1,049 miles long in honor of Alaska, the 49th state, the trail actually encompasses more than 1,150 miles of rough terrain.
- Both in 1967 and in 1969, shorter races were conducted on part of the present-day Iditarod Trail, before the official race was launched in 1974.

# INUIT GLOSSARY

**Anniu:** falling snow

**Asujutilli:** modern Inuit greeting; no direct translation

**Ikajunnga! (Eekah-yoo-nnga!):** Help!

**Li (Ee):** Yes

**Aakka or aagaa (Ah-ka or Ah-ga):** No

**Quanuippit? (Khah-nweep-peet?):** How are you?

**Qiuliqtunga (Khiu-lirk-toonga):** I am cold.

**Kaaktunga (Kaak-toonga):** I am hungry.

**Qujannamiik (Khoo-yannah-meek):** Thank you.

**Ilaali (E-laah-li):** You are welcome.

**Tavvauvutit (Tub-vow-voo-teet)** Good-bye (to you)

**Tavvauvusi (Tub-vow-voo-see):** Good-bye (to all)

**Uvanga:** my name is

# GLOSSARY

 **blustery:** blowing in violent and abrupt bursts

 **ceremonial:** related to a formal act of observance or ritual

**escapade:** adventure, or an exciting undertaking

 **fluctuates:** moves in a wavelike pattern

 **frontier:** a wilderness at the edge of a settled area of a country

**replenished:** filled something that had previously been emptied

**scowling:** sullen or unfriendly in appearance

**tandem:** a setup in which two things are arranged one behind the other

*Enjoy this exciting excerpt from:*

# THE MYSTERY AT KILL DEVIL HILLS

## 1
## MAN WILL NEVER FLY

Grant, Christina, Mimi and Papa stood and looked at the little red airplane. It had *My Girl* written on the side in cursive.

"Are we all packed?" Papa asked.

"Everything's stowed away, captain," said Mimi.

Grant and Christina giggled. Their grandfather had only recently gotten his pilot's license and was flying them to North Carolina for the big 100th anniversary of the First Flight celebration. It was going to be a BIG DEAL. Her grandmother had been writing books about the Wright brothers' incredible first manned flight for more than a year.

"Then all aboard!" Papa said.

"Don't you have your planes and your trains all mixed up?" Christina teased Papa.

Papa roared with laughter. "Planes, trains, automobiles, camels, donkeys, rickshaws—whatever it takes, we're going to be in Kill Devil Hills in time for the whole shebang," he promised.

The "whole shebang" was supposed to be everything you could imagine to celebrate the "First Flight." The president of the United States was coming. So was the aircraft carrier *Kitty Hawk*. There was going to be a big flyover of all kinds of aircraft—including old-fashioned barnstormers, as well as the latest spy planes! And, most special, a replica of *Flyer*, Orville and Wilbur Wright's first real airplane, was going to be flown over the sand dunes at Kill Devil Hills.

Of course, thought Christina, Mimi was most excited about the Black and White "First Flight" Ball! Her ball gown was beautiful—all black satin with white trim and sparkly crystal stones. She swore she was going to wear red shoes beneath it, for good luck. Christina sure wished *she* was going to the ball. She looked over at Grant who was strapped in and wide-eyed. He had never flown in a plane this small before, and he looked a little scared.

"It's ok, Grant," Christina told her younger brother, who was seven.  Christina was nine and liked to think she had seen it all, although she knew she had not.  However, she *had* seen a lot since she and her brother often gallivanted across the United States with their grandparents.  Mimi wrote mystery books for kids and often included her grandchildren, their friends, and members of her Carole Marsh Mysteries fan club in the books.

They had been a lot of cool places, always having fun . . . and almost always getting in trouble before it was over with.  Of course, Mimi usually put all that in the books, so it was ok.  She called it "research."  Grant and Christina called it getting out of school with a neat excuse!

On this trip to the Outer Banks of North Carolina, they were going to meet up with their Tarheel cousins Alex and Griffin.  Alex (short for Alexis) was almost 13 and Griffin was 10.  They were a lot of fun to be around.  Christina was envious that they got to live at the beach year-round.  They always had tans and windblown hair.  They knew how to surf and hang glide and all of that beachy keen stuff.  Christina hoped they would teach her some of that this year.  She was not used to going to the beach in the winter, though.  Why couldn't

Orville and Wilbur have made their famous first flight in the summer, she thought.

Suddenly, Papa revved the engines and the shiny propellers began to spin. The Halloween orange windsock at Falcon Field seemed to satisfy Papa that it was "all systems go." Christina thought her grandfather would have made a good astronaut. When she told him that, he said, "I might yet, kiddo!"

They waved goodbye to their family—Mom, Dad, Uncle Michael, Aunt Cassidy, and their shiny, pink, new baby girl, Avery Elizabeth. Christina couldn't wait until Avery—or "Duckie," as Mimi called her because she had so many outfits with ducks on them, was old enough to join them on trips like this.

As the little plane began to speed across the tarmac, Grant grabbed his sister by the hand. "Hey," he yelled over the noise of the engine. "Don't Mimi and Papa belong to the Man Will Never Fly Society?"

"Yes," Christina screamed back at him. The adults in front could not even hear them.

"Then," said Grant, "if man will never fly, what are we doing in this contraption?"

Christina laughed. "Oh, Grant, you've flown on airplanes before. Lots of times."

"I kknow," said Grant, his voice stuttering as the plane's wheels seemed to bounce across the runway. "Bbut they were BIG. This thing ffeels llike a rrocking hhorse."

Christina held her brother's hand tighter as the airplane suddenly swooshed smoothly up into the air. A little turbulence rocked them left and right as they pulled up into the sky. As Papa banked into a turn over the beautiful forested city where they lived—Peachtree City, Georgia—Grant seemed to relax. He let his sister's hand drop and stretched and yawned as though the takeoff had been a piece of cake.

"I guess man *will* fly," Grant admitted.

"Well, thousands of people are sure counting on it in North Carolina this week," Christina said, fishing around in her backpack for some pretzels.

As he leveled the airplane, Papa glanced back at his two grandchildren. "Orville and Wilbur, here we come!" he said.

Everyone, including Mimi, laughed. That's because they had no way of knowing that they were flying into the strangest mystery they had ever encountered, and that the fate of the BIG DEAL celebration would be up to four kids.

*Enjoy this exciting excerpt from:*

# THE MYSTERY ON THE FREEDOM TRAIL

## 1
## WHAT IN THE WORLD IS A BM ANYWAY?

"Boston is a long way from Georgia," Christina mused as she read the curious white note with the red lining once again. "I guess we'd have to take an airplane."

Christina Yother, 9, a fourth-grader in Peachtree City, Georgia, her brother, Grant, 7, and their Grandmother Mimi stood around the bright red mailbox. They ignored the bills, advertisements, and the little box of free detergent stuffed in the mailbox to concentrate on the invitation to visit Boston. The invitation read:

Mimi,

You and your two delightful grandchildren are invited to visit us during the big BM! Cousins Derian and C.F. will enjoy showing the kids Bean Town! Let me know ASAP. Patriots' Day is coming soon, you know!

> Love,
> Emma

Mimi tapped the note with her bright red fingernail. "I guess Patriots' Day *is* coming soon. Today is the last day of March. She could have given us a little more notice."

Of course, Christina knew that didn't really matter to her Grandmother Mimi. She was not like most grandmothers. She wasn't really like a grandmother at all. She had bright blond hair, wore all the latest sparkly clothes, was the CEO of her own company, and took off for parts unknown at a moment's notice.

"Aunt Emma sure likes exclamation points," observed Christina. "Just like you, Mimi!"

"You bet!" said Mimi, giving her granddaughter's silky, chestnut-colored hair a tousle. "I'm the Exclamation Mark Queen!" She looked down at Grant who was fingering the corner of the invitation. He looked very serious. "What's wrong, Grant?" asked Mimi.

Even standing on the curb, Grant was small. His blue eyes seemed the biggest part of him. He looked up at his grandmother. "Well, for one thing, Aunt Emma sure uses a lot of letters instead of words. What does ASAP stand for?"

Christina knew that one. (Of course, she always did!) "It means As Soon As Possible—right, Mimi?"

"That's right," said Mimi. "You can say A-S-A-P, or say it like a word—asap."

"Then I hate to be a sap and ask the next question," said Grant with a sigh.

"What's that?" asked Mimi. "There are no dumb questions, you know."

Grant slid off the curb, looking littler than ever. "It's not the question that bothers me . . . it's the possible answer. I mean what *is* a big BM?"

Mimi laughed. "Not what you apparently think it means! The BM is the Boston Marathon. It's the biggest deal in Boston each year. People come from all over the world to run in this race."

"Oh," Grant said with a grin. He looked relieved, and so did his sister. "So it's like the Peachtree Road Race on the 4th of July?"

"Sort of," said Mimi, folding the note and stuffing it back in its envelope. "Only the Boston Marathon is the oldest marathon in America, so it's really special. It has an incredible history!"

Christina and Grant grabbed one another and groaned. Oh, no! When Mimi said the word *history*, they knew they would be in for a big, long tale of everything about everything. But not this time. She ignored her grandkids' dramatic groaning and headed up the driveway for the house.

Christina chased her, running beneath the overhang of magnolia limbs over the azalea-lined path of pink and purple blooms. "Are we going?"

Grant chased Christina. "Wait up, you two!" he pleaded. He took a shortcut across the wide green lawn, weaving (against Mimi's rules) through the forest of pampas grass spewing fountains of white, feathery spikes. "Are we going?" he begged.

On the front porch, Mimi plopped down in the big, white Victorian rocking chair. She pulled out her cell phone from her jacket pocket. Grant and Christina piled into the rocker beside her. "Are we?  Are we?!" they hissed, as Mimi dialed the number.  They held their breath until they heard her say, "Emma?  We're coming to the Big BM!"

After Mimi hung up the phone, she jiggled the other rocking chair, causing the two kids to giggle.  "What's wrong, Grant?" she asked.  "You still don't look happy!"

Grant looked at his grandmother thoughtfully.  "If we go to Boston, do we get to eat anything beside beans?"